Samuel W. Hall

Sunshine and Moonlight

With, also, a Flash of Comets, Meteors and Shooting Stars, and a Twinkle

of Starlight

Samuel W. Hall

Sunshine and Moonlight
With, also, a Flash of Comets, Meteors and Shooting Stars, and a Twinkle of Starlight

ISBN/EAN: 9783337255121

Printed in Europe, USA, Canada, Australia, Japan

Cover: Foto ©Andreas Hilbeck / pixelio.de

More available books at **www.hansebooks.com**

AN OBSERVATORY.

SUNSHINE

AND

MOONLIGHT

WITH, ALSO,

A FLASH OF COMETS, METEORS AND SHOOTING STARS,
AND A TWINKLE OF STARLIGHT.

How the Boys and Girls had a Holiday "Outing," at Home.

BY

OF THE GREAT ROCK ISLAND ROUTE.

Respectfully Dedicated to the Boys and Girls of America, by the
CHICAGO, ROCK ISLAND & PACIFIC RAILWAY.

CHICAGO:
STROMBERG, ALLEN & CO., PRINTERS.
1889.

"In the beginning GOD created the heaven and the earth.

And the earth was without form, and void; and darkness was upon the face of the deep. And the Spirit of GOD moved upon the face of the deep.

And GOD said, Let there be light : and there was light.

And GOD saw the light that it was good : and GOD divided the light from the darkness.

And GOD called the light Day and the darkness he called Night.

* * * * *

And GOD said, Let there be lights in the firmament of the heaven to divide the day from the night; and let them be for signs, and for seasons, and for days and for years :

And let them be for lights in the firmament of the heaven to give light upon the earth : and it was so.

And GOD made two great lights, the greater light to rule the day, and the lesser light to rule the night : he made the stars also.

And GOD set them in the firmament of the heaven to give light upon the earth,

And to rule over the day and over the night, and to divide the light from the darkness : and GOD saw that it was good."—*Genesis 1.*

* * * * * * *

"The heavens declare the glory of GOD, and the firmament showeth his handiwork.

Day unto day uttereth speech, and night unto night showeth knowledge."—*Psalm 19 : 1, 2.*

PREFACE.

WITH the approach, again, of the holiday season, come thoughts of the little people, and of what can be done to make their Christmas any more merry or their New Year any more happy. As usual, "A MAN" of the GREAT ROCK ISLAND ROUTE (though by no means aspiring to rival or supplant the children's truest friend—him of the "eight tiny reindeer") brings his little offering to his little friends, north, south, east and west, and begs they will accept it, with his best wishes for their happiness during not only the holiday time, but throughout the coming year.

In making a rather wide departure from the line of his former efforts of this kind, "A MAN" trusts that his work will be, at least, no less acceptable than has that which has already been offered. It is his wish that this little volume, the sixth of the series, may not only please and entertain, in a measure, those who may chance to read it, but that it may awaken in some of them, at least, a strong desire to know more of these things; that it may lead them to seek a fuller knowledge of GOD's works and ways as shown, not alone in the wonders of the heavens, but in the manifold wonders everywhere about us, on and in the earth, as well,—for it is literally a "world of wonders." "A MAN" would have his little books to accomplish something in the way of supplanting the trashy and vicious literature, now so freely offered to young people, with something far better, by pointing out to his young friends some of the paths along which they may most pleasantly and profitably travel.

As with former issues, the indulgence of older and more critical readers is asked touching the matters of frequent repetitions, odd phraseology, etc., made necessary by the nature of the work; to present the wonderful truths of astronomy so that little folks may understand them even fairly well, is no light task. The aim has been to present elementary facts as plainly as possible.

With the wish, again, for all my little friends, that they may have, this season, another most "Merry Christmas" and most "Happy New Year," I remain, as ever,

Your friend,

ACKNOWLEDGMENT.

WHILE making a general acknowledgment of the assistance received from various sources in the preparation of this little book, "A Man" would make especial mention of his very great indebtedness to Prof. Lewis Swift, Director of Warner Observatory, Rochester, N. Y., for most valued assistance, freely tendered, in both the matters of the preparation of the text and its illustration; also, in connection with the last-mentioned matter, to Messrs. A. S. Barnes & Co., Publishers, New York, for the privilege of reproducing in these pages a number of the most beautiful and valuable illustrations from one of their educational text-books—Steele's Astronomy.

I.

MISS INQUISITIVE'S LETTER AND "A MAN'S" SOLILOQUY

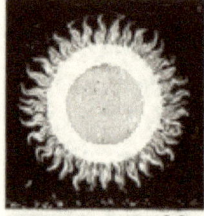

HO! here's a dainty little missive, hidden among these other, big letters. I wonder—ah, yes, from Miss Inquisitive, I see; one glance at the address tells me that. I declare, even her writing wears, to me, an inquiring expression, as it were. That *g*, now, is a veritable interrogation point, staring at me from the paper exactly as if it is expecting an answer, and is not altogether pleased at my delay in giving it. Of course, this is all fancy, but anyhow I shall have some fun at her expense, in regard to the matter, next time I see her.

·Well, I wonder what mischief her ladyship has under way, now; there's something in hand, I venture to say. I haven't been honored with a letter from her since she was engaged in arranging that surprise for Ned's birthday; and, by the way, I haven't seen her since that long-to-be-remembered occasion—an unusually long time, I declare! But whatever this may mean, I certainly am glad to hear from her, again; she's a good girl, with all her pranks and question-asking, and it does me good even to hear from her by letter, although I would be much more pleased had she delivered her message in person. I wonder what she *does* want, anyhow. I suppose I shall have to grant her request, in any case, 'even to the half of my kingdom', as it were, since it is next to impossible to prevent myself from agreeing to anything she suggests. I must say for her, however, that I never have had to regret such a course in the past, for she has as good a little heart as she has a busy little head, and none of her plans, mischievous as some of them are, occasionally, have in them anything of unpleasantness for anybody; on the contrary, they all have in view the giving of pleasure to all concerned. It is no wonder everybody likes her. I'd like to know just what—but, dear me! I can find out more quickly by opening her letter than by turning it over in my hands and reading my name and address right and left, and up and down, as I've been doing for five minutes. Let's see, then.

Dear me! sick, is she? Too bad! too bad! Ah, yes—'*I would have been in to see you last Saturday, if mamma had not been afraid to let me go.*' I thought it strange she hadn't been here, poor thing! I knew she hadn't forgotten me. What's this?—'*like to have you come over to see me, some day soon, as I want to talk to you about our usual holiday trip.*'—

Oh-h, yes, I had n't thought of that matter, yet; that is why she writes to me, eh?—'*I'm afraid—indeed, I know—that I shall not be able to go with you this time. I am not* VERY *sick, and do not at all feel as if I need be kept in the house; but mamma and papa and old Doctor Pillsbury all tell me I must—and so I must. They say it is not because I am so very sick now, but it is to prevent me from getting very sick, and of course they know more than I do about what sick people should do to get well. So, I shall have to stay at home, this time; but I hope the rest of you will have a grand good time.*'—Dear, dear! what a good little soul she is; I don't believe I ever have half appreciated her goodness. But what else does she say?—'*So, please come over, soon, for even if I can't go, I would so much like to help plan something for your trip. I don't think I could help much in planning the kind of trip to take, or where to go, but perhaps I may be able to do something, in some way, to make the trip more pleasant for some of you, or all of you, maybe. Do you think I could?*'—Do I think so? Well, now, I just *do* think so—'*Nell and Ned and all the rest, I guess, are coming to see me to-morrow, I hear, and I would be so pleased to have you here, too. I think, too, it would be a good time to arrange for our—I mean your—trip, wherever you may go. So, please come, if you can; you may be sure it will please us all, and especially*

Your little friend,

"*Interrogation Point.*"'

Did I ever hear the like?—'Interrogation Point!' I called her that over at Ned's, that evening, when she was teasing and puzzling me with all kinds of queer questions about the big moon that was shining so brightly—poor little thing!

Well, I must arrange to go over and see her, and meet my other young friends, to-morrow. So, I'm to be called upon to head another holiday excursion party, it seems. But what in the world shall it be like?—where shall we go? I'm sure I don't know, now; but some good plan may be thought of, to-morrow. We've been among the oil and gas wells; have visited the coal and coke regions, and explored the mines; have also been among the iron mines and through the great iron and steel works of different kinds, and where to go, this year, is a puzzling question. I think I shall have to throw the matter of arranging for our trip upon the youngsters, themselves, as I have done for the last two years; the outcome was very satisfactory to all of us, in both those instances, and I doubt not would be so in this one, also. We might, still ascending the scale of mineral products, next visit the gold and silver mines of the far West—the Rocky mountain and Pacific coast regions; indeed, that seems to me a pretty good idea. I know all would enjoy it, and Miss Inquis—ah, I forget, she could n't go with us, poor girl, and without her—dear me, it's *too* bad! But then, of course, she cannot go with us, no matter where we may go; so that, after all, it would make no difference to her, in one sense, whether we visit Maine or California. But I do wish she could go with us, or that we could arrange matters so as to give her a fair share of the enjoyment we may find—at least, more than she would be expected to have, penned up in her room while all her young friends are hundreds of miles away, enjoying all kinds of strange and interesting sights and experiences. But what can be done in the matter? Let me see; let—me—see. Oh, dear! I'll have to give it up, for the present, I see, and trust to the future to have things all come out right.

Well, I will answer these letters—which I had nearly forgotten—and arrange everything so that I shall not have to disappoint the sick girl and my other little friends, to-morrow."

II.

THE MEETING: PLANS AND PLANS—THE ONE ADOPTED.

"Well, well, this is a fine party, to be sure.— Oh, I'm very well, thank you—very well, indeed; how are you, all? All well, eh?—and happy, too, it seems. Ah, here's the sick girl—how are you, to-day, young lady? So you're better, to-day; that's good, and I'm glad to hear it, you may be sure. You certainly are having a very good time, too, for a sick girl, from all appearances. If it were not that you are so pale and rather thin, and perhaps just a *very little* less enthusiastic— I won't say boisterous—in your greeting, one would hardly pick you out as the sick girl of the party. What? Ha-ha-ha! bad as ever, I declare. I was wondering, on my way over, whether your sickness had affected your query-box, but it has n't, I see. It's my opinion that it will be a very severe sickness that will stop the flow of your questions, and I shall be really alarmed when such a point is reached; as it is, I have no present fears. But, jesting aside, I am sorry to find you sick, at all; but at the same time very glad, indeed, to find your sickness no more serious than this—and as you tell me, find you better, to-day, than you have been. I have no doubt you are feeling better than you otherwise would on account of the presence of this jolly crowd; one could really afford to be just a little sick, if necessary, for the sake of the fun to be had from such a company as this.

By the way, Ned, how are you and Tom succeeding with your perpetual motion machine? Ha, ha!—just one or two little things needed yet, eh? Well, I sincerely trust you will find them; if you do, fame and fortune will certainly be yours, as these one or two little things have been anxiously hunted for by the great multitude of inventors who have puzzled their brains over the matter, before you took it up.   But hammer away, no harm can come of it, anyway, and you may gain some valuable practical knowledge of mechanics.   Who knows but that, as the outcome of your present struggle, the world may be astonished, somewhere in coming years, by some wonderful and valuable inventions.   You haven't forgotten Watt and the tea-kettle, I'm sure.   So, work away; you might be far more poorly employed.

Say, Nell, how are you getting along with that pair—Oh, my! didn't I nearly let out a secret?   I forgot about the necessity for keeping certain things quiet at this time of the year.   However, I'll try to keep my tongue still, hereafter—or, at least, not point it in your direction again.

How is mamma, Bess?—and little 'Blossom'?   And how are all the mammas and papas and wee people?   Glad to hear it; everybody is well, it seems, but this poor girl, here,—but who, I am compelled to say, doesn't seem to be suffering much at this particular time.

What were you doing when I was coming up the steps?   Such a tumult of shouts and laughter I have n't heard since we were all over at Ned's.   Another of Joe's puns?   We'll have to do something with that young gentleman, I'm afraid; he's getting entirely too bright for the rest of us.   We must suppress him, and that soon, too, in self-defense.

Well, what is the programme for this afternoon?—blind-man's buff to begin with, I suppose, with me for the first blind-man, as usual.   Then, I suppose,—Oho! Miss Inquisitive has been putting mischief into your heads, I see; she's not too sick to do that, it seems.   So, excursion is the only cry—no one seems to care for games, strange to say.   I suppose, then, I may as well fall right in with your demands; many former experiences have taught me the wisdom of doing so without a murmur.   Now, what have you to propose?—Nothing! well, you are a bright set of youngsters, to be sure!   Do you call it fair now, I want to ask, to invite me to *help you* do something and then as much as tell me I must do it *all myself?*—and then add insult to injury by laughing uproariously at my protest against such ill-usage!   I would consider myself very badly treated if I did n't know the party so well.   So, it seems, you stand precisely where you have stood a number of times before, knowing very well, indeed, that you want to go on a holiday trip, but having not even the faintest idea as to where you want to go—a very interesting but not very satisfactory state of affairs, I must say.

Under such circumstances, I propose to do exactly as I did last year, and the year before—let you hunt up a plan, yourselves.   No doubt you all recollect how I put you to work, and kept you thinking as hard as you knew how until, through Miss Inquisitive's unexpected—and at the time, utterly out-of-place questions—we were led to the adoption of the right plan, as it proved, in each instance; so, just get to work again and rack your brains, if need be, in your efforts to hit upon what will suit us most in the matter of this year's trip.   I will say at the outset that I am very sorry that,—as you are all aware, no doubt,—Miss Inquisitive cannot leave home, and, of course, cannot be with us on our trip. Now, my idea of the best plan is, one that shall in some way include our sick member in its pleasures and benefits—just how, we shall have to decide. Even if we have to give up the idea of going—Now, Miss, you just keep quiet—it isn't good for sick people to talk too much, you know; we'll have our own way, this time—if only we can find out just what it is. Well, we are now ready to listen to anyone who has a plan to offer— and I promise an extra box of your own selection of Christmas candy to the one who presents the plan which we shall adopt. To work, then, all the rest of you, while I have a little talk with the sick girl, who is excused from work, this time.

Now, young lady, what ails you, anyway?—been trying to bottle up some questions instead of asking them, just to see whether you could do it, and now find yourself sick as the result?—Oh, a severe cold, is it? I am glad it is nothing necessarily serious or alarming, but something from which, with the care you are receiving, we may hope to have you speedily recover.

Well, Nell, you're first, anyway; what have you to propose?—A pretty good idea, young lady, I must say. There is certainly much of interest to be seen in the various kinds of mills and factories which we have never yet visited, here at home; and, besides, Miss Inquisitive might be able to be with us at least a part of the time.

What! Tom, have you a plan, too? I thought you were doing some extra deep thinking. What is it, then?—Ha-ha!—an original idea, surely; no wonder it caused such a shout. A *Christmas* excursion to the Mammoth Cave, on the *Fourth of July*, would certainly possess a large degree of novelty to say the least; while the idea of such a post-ponement of our trip, on Miss Inquisitive's account, speaks much for your kindness of heart. The trip itself would no doubt be a pleasant one, and we might reasonably hope for Miss Inquisitive's presence on that occasion. We'll consider the suggestion, anyway, Tom. Bess, you make a list of the plans as offered.

Ha-ha-ha! a seasonable suggestion, Ned, very, and quite as novel as Tom's. A trip to the north pole, or at least in that direction, instead of to the Mammoth Cave, in midsummer, might be more to the taste of some of you, I'll admit.—There, there, Joe, that will do, sir; I fancy your joke will throw a chill over the meeting more piercing than Ned's suggestion has. Anyway, you seem to stand very greatly in need of some-thing of the kind, to check the growth of your budding genius in a certain direction. We are ready, now, for plan No. 4—and as no one seems to have it ready to offer, I will take up my talk with the sick girl; when you're ready, let me hear from you.

Now, young lady, let us see if we can steal a few minutes' talk, again.—Dear me! have you another lot of moon-questions to ask me? I must say that when once you get fairly started upon a subject you know no rest until you have gone to the bottom of it—or the top of it, as the case may be. What an odd question—how thick is the moon? Still, since I think of it, it is quite a natural question, after all, viewing the moon as it seems you have always viewed it—simply as a round, flat object. The moon, however, is not a flat thing, as it appears when we look at it, but is round like this ball—as our earth itself is, you know. So, you see, we cannot speak of the moon as being thick, like a cheese or a grindstone, but we would speak of its diameter or distance through the center, just as we speak of the earth's diameter. So—How do I know it is round? Now, there you go, again, as naturally as ever—one question on top of another! Why if I should n't object, you would run right on. I'm pretty sure, skipping nimbly from one point to another, until I should have been dragged all over the field of moon knowledge—new moons, quarters, full moons, tides, eclipses, etc.—Oh, dear me, child! I could n't do all that; would n't have time for that alone, not to mention the other and very important matter which we have on hand, just now.— Some evening? Ye-es, I think I might—only it will take several evenings to tell all you would want to know, and—Ah, I have it!—I have it! Here youngsters, all of you, I have a plan to offer,—No. 4 on your list, Bess,—and you can then go to work, again, thinking up others.

How would you like to take a trip to the moon, taking Miss Inquisitive w¹ h us? Now, what am I to understand by such a startling 'Oh-h-!.' as that, from all of you? Does it mean 'Oh, *yes*, or 'Oh, *no*'?— Do I mean it? Why, to be sure—in a kind of way: and the voyage would be neither so chilly nor dangerous as a trip to the pole. No, Tom, not in a balloon or air ship; we'll go—in case we decide to do so, at all— we'll go in this room of Miss Inquisitive's which, besides being much more cozy and comfortable than an air ship, is a considerably safer vessel, inasmuch as we shall remain securely anchored here in this yard while making our voyage. Hold—hold! not more than four or five at a time, if you please. Now, if you'll all keep quiet long enough—not a single question to be asked—I'll tell you what I mean.

To begin with, I must state that I do not mean that we shall actually go to the moon—that, as some of you may know, is impossible. What I have in mind, however, is this: Instead of going away from home, as has been our custom for several years, I would suggest—mind, I only suggest it, and you can do as you please about it—I would suggest that, since Miss Inquisitive cannot leave her home, we gather here in her room in the evenings, and have some talks about the moon, and possibly, about some of the other heavenly bodies, as the sun, moon, stars, etc., are called. I think I can say for our sick girl, that this would be, to her, an especially enjoyable arrangement, indeed; as, first, she would have you all here with her so often, and, secondly, she would have an opportunity to learn a little more, perhaps, about a subject which, I happen to know, has been interesting her very much ever since the night of our party at Tom's. Of course, she and all of you will learn much more about the matters of which I might speak, when you are older and take up the study of astronomy,—as the science of the stars, etc., is called; but it will do no harm to talk about them now, and may even do some good, as I have found, in my own experience, that many things learned in this or some similar way have been better learned— that is, have been more easily, fully and clearly understood, and so are more likely to be always remembered—than when learned in the manner in which things are too often learned at school.

Now, I have given you my plan, in a general way; we are ready for others to be offered, and when all are in we will vote upon them to decide which shall be adopted. I said *my* plan, but I must take that back and waive all claims to it, and give the credit to Miss Inquisitive, who really brought it out by her ques—Oh, yes, you did, ma'am, and you must n't try to deny it. Now, who's ready with another plan?

What!—*all* in favor of the moon trip! Don't you want to go to the Mammoth Cave, Tom?—nor you, Ned, to the north pole? Well, it seems that the matter has been settled in short order. To Miss Inquisitive, then, belongs the credit for suggesting our plan of operations for three successive years. And I'm sure you all like her too much to be the least bit jealous about the matter; while as for the young lady, herself, she will wear her increasing honors very lightly, I'm sure, and will not become too proud to look at or speak to the rest of us who have never gained such distinction. And I will take this opportunity to say for her, further, that, while I am sure she will be highly delighted with the carrying out of the plan we have just adopted, she would, in her real unselfishness, prefer that we should adopt some other plan which would give all the rest of us our customary excursion. Indeed, she wrote me, only yesterday, in regard to the matter, saying she would be unable to go with us on our trip, but seeming very anxious that the rest of us should go and should have a splendid time. Oh, she's as kind-hearted as she is—ahem!—is inquisitive; that's saying a great deal for her kind-heartedness, isn't it, now?

Well, now that this matter is settled, I must be off. We will meet here Christmas afternoon to begin our astronomical talks,—there's a good big word for you to hunt up in your new dictionary, Ned. In the meantime, I will map out some kind of plan of operations. Well, good by, young lady,—take good care of yourself, mind; good by, all of you, good by—good by!"

III

A CHRISTMAS PARTY WHERE LITTLE PEOPLE DEAL WITH BIG SUBJECTS.

"Merry Christmas, youngsters! merry Christmas, to all of you!—and especially to you, Miss Inquisitive, who are supposed to be more particularly in need of good cheer. It seems to me, however, that you are to be considered, in many respects, the most fortunate one among us. I trust you all have most fully enjoyed the day; that it has brought to you showers of presents and pleasures.—Oh, don't mention that, please; you deserved it, anyway. And, by the way, I must tell you about something very useful and beautiful which in some most mysterious way crept into my room while I was out yesterday, or last night, and was found by me, this morning.—Oh, yes; I have an idea—and a very correct one, I think—as to where it came from, if not as to how it got into the place in which it was found. But while I have my suspicions as to who are concerned in the matter, I shall keep quiet, and some day one of the guilty persons may confess or may accidentally let the secret out. By that time I may be ready to forgive them, as, to tell the truth, I am really very much pleased with the article found, and in the meantime shall make good use of it,—here it is, you see.—Oh, yes, indeed, its very handsome; did any of you ever see anything just like it—*exactly* like it? H-m-m, yes—I supposed some of you had, likely.

Much better, to-day, are you, young lady? Well, I don't wonder at it, at all; why, I feel so myself, although I am sure I was perfectly well, before I came in. Queer, isn't it? And as for the rest of you, if you are not perfectly well and happy, too, this afternoon, your faces do not tell the truth about your feelings.—Come, now, Joe, no joking about such matters, sir; we'll get nothing done if you keep up such an uproar with your smart remarks.

Attention, everybody! I suppose we are to begin our talks, this afternoon, according to agreement; if so, we must get to work, at once. I will, by virtue of age and size, lay claim to, and take possession of, this big easy chair, and try to fill it; the sick girl, here, by virtue of her many claims, in addition to her illness, shall occupy the seat of honor, here; and the rest of you—well, we'll let you do as the lesser politicians have to do under somewhat similar circumstances—take what is left and make the best of it. However, there is no especial hardship about the matter, in this case; so gather around us, here, to suit yourselves, and we'll see what is to be done.

Since our last meeting, here, I have been giving some thought, according to promise, to the matter of a plan of procedure, trying to decide upon what points should be considered, in what order, etc.; but I have not succeeded in this very much to my own satisfaction, as it is by no means an easy task, I assure you. So, I have given up the idea of following any set plan—since I have not been able to arrange one— and while I shall keep in mind some of the principal points to be spoken of, and shall try to introduce them in some kind of order, we shall let others take their turn just as they happen to present themselves by reason of your questions, or otherwise.

I should state, at the outset, that the science of *astronomy*, as we term the study of the sun, moon, stars and other heavenly bodies, is probably the oldest of all sciences. From the earliest times man has studied these bodies and their movements, the ancient Egyptians, Chaldeans and other peoples being great astronomers in their day, though knowing little as compared with the knowledge we have, to-day, touching these matters. It is, indeed, only within the last three or four hundred years that the great truths of astronomy have been discovered and given to the world by such men as Copernicus, Kepler, Galileo, Newton, Herschel and others, down to the many illustrious names of the present day,—though we are indebted to the ancient astronomers, of course, for the valuable beginning they made for us. At the present day, the astronomer enjoys advantages of which earlier students of the heavens neither knew nor dreamed. Buildings known as *observatories* are prepared for the especial use of astronomers, within which are to be found many valuable and curious instruments designed to aid them in their great work, the principal one being one or more telescopes of great size and power, which apparently bring the far distant bodies to within a short distance of the observer, and enable him to see what could never be seen by the eye alone, besides which there are various instruments, most accurately constructed, used to make various measurements, etc.

While it was about the moon in particular that Miss Inquisitive wanted to know so many things, I have concluded to first give you some information in regard to the sun, as being the more important body— although it may be that some of you share the opinion of the man who gave more credit to the moon because, as he argued, it gives us light at night, when we need it, while the sun gives us light by day, when we have plenty of light without it.—Your idea, too, is it, Joe? Ha-ha! you'll find the laugh is against you, for once, young man, when we get a little further along in our talk. Yes, the sun—Joe and the man of the story to the contrary, notwithstanding, as the lawyers say—the sun is of much greater relative importance than the moon, it being, indeed, the center of the whole solar system, as we—Yes—yes—yes! I'll explain, if you'll give me a chance. To tell the truth, I should have begun with an explanation of what is meant by the solar system, before taking up the sun, moon or other members of that system; so, we will start again.

GENERAL VIEW OF INSIDE OF OBSERVATORY,

The solar system is—now, how *shall* I go to work to explain this to you youngsters? It's a rather large subject, you'll discover, and you'll have to put everything else out of your heads, for the time, in order to get it all in comfortably and in good order,—for you will find, too, that it is very important that order be observed in the solar system, even in our minds.

I'll start again. You all know that the earth—the world in which or on which we live—is a round body—a large body, too, being, as some of you could tell me, about 25,000 miles in circumference, or the distance around it, and about 8,000 miles in diameter, or the distance through its center. Now, the solar system as it is termed is made up of a number of great round bodies—other worlds they are—like our earth, all constantly moving around the sun. The Latin name for sun is *sol*, from which we get the word *solar*, meaning relating to or belonging to the sun, or *sol*. Now, the sun, earth and these other bodies of which I have spoken, taken together, form a system of worlds; and as all the others move around the sun and have their movements controlled by it, and get their light and heat from it, the whole system of bodies is called the *solar* system—that is, the system of the sun. I will only mention, here, that the thousands of stars which we can easily see, and the almost countless thousands which we can see only by the use of powerful telescopes, so far away are they, are also great suns, each forming a part of almost countless other systems like the one to which our sun and world belong.

To return to our system, again, I will say that of the other worlds belonging to it some are smaller than our earth, while some of them are much larger—many times larger, indeed.—Oh, no, Joe, there's no mistake about that; I have the best of authority for that statement— even if you never have seen any other world larger than this one. However, I'm pretty sure you have seen several of them.—Sure you never did, eh? Ha-ha! next to your weakness for puns and jokes, your distinguishing trait is your stick-to-it quality in the matter of an opinion—not a bad quality, perhaps, provided you always retain your perfect willingness to surrender when you find there is no use to argue any longer. I think you have seen some of these other bodies belonging to the solar system, though, of course, not knowing they belonged to it; and if you will go to the window with me, after the stars have come out, I may be able to point out one or two of these worlds so that you can recognize them and be able to point them out, hereafter, to other persons.—Oh, no, not all of the stars; they are, indeed, all suns or worlds, as I have already told you, but only a few of all we can see belong to our system of worlds,—the solar system. These few other worlds which belong to our system we call *planets*.

Little things? No, indeed; some of them, as I told you a moment ago, are very many times larger than our own world. The reason they appear so small to us—mere bright specks in the sky—is, they are so far away—millions upon millions of miles out in space.—Oh, dear me! Miss Inquisitive, that's a dreadful question you're asking: What is space? Why, space is—is—I wish you would n't ask such questions, young lady —space is—well, it is *room;* that's Webster's definition, I believe, and I'm entirely too modest, you know, to think myself able to improve upon his work. By room, as used in this definition, we mean the space in which—ha-ha-ha, you certainly have caught me, Ned; to tell you that space is room, and then to try to explain that by saying room is space, certainly is 'coming out at about the same place at which I started in.' Well, I'll try it again.

Let us suppose that we should take a balloon or an air ship and sail away from the earth, say, a thousand miles. It is utterly impossible for us or anybody else to do this, I should tell you; but we will suppose that we can do it—that we have done it; that we have left the earth and sailed away through the air, beyond the clouds, and still on and on, until we are now a thousand miles or more from our homes on the earth. What would surround us? We would be floating in—what? No, not air; I was expecting such an answer, however, though thinking it possible some of you might catch the thought I had in mind. Your answer is a very natural one, but a wrong one, however. There would not be air about us, there, as there is here upon the earth, or close to it. The air, or atmosphere, which we breathe and which is everywhere on the earth, extends upward or outward from the earth only a short distance, comparatively; it completely surrounds the earth, of course, in a layer which according to some learned men, is less than 50 miles in thickness,—that is, in height above the earth's surface,—while by others it is thought to be perhaps as much as 500 miles in thickness, or height. But beyond this limit, whether it be 50 or 500 miles, there is no air; so, out where we are in our balloon, as we are supposing, and extending still beyond and around us, on and on endlessly, boundlessly, there is a great void or emptiness, and it is this vast emptiness that is called *space.* I have called it a vast emptiness, but it is not so, strictly speaking, since it contains, though separated each from each by immense distances, thousands, yes, millions, of worlds!—our own world and the others which belong to the solar system, and the countless number known to us as the stars. Yet it is, for the most part, emptiness, as we view it; for, while fairly swarming with worlds, these each occupy but a small part of it, with a great ·expanse of this emptiness—millions upon millions of miles—lying between them. Yes, they do appear to be very close together, Ned, as we look at them on a clear, beautiful night, but this apparent closeness is due to their wonderful distance from us; if we could visit them, passing from one to the other, you would soon discover how greatly mistaken you are in supposing them close to each other. The fact is this, that while the distance of all is so great that they appear to be side by side in the heavens, they are separated by immense distances from each other, not only to the right or left, or above or below, as we view them, but some of them are many billions and others trillions of miles beyond, or as we may say, back of, the others!—Big figures, indeed, Ned,—much more astonishing than what we considered big figures in regard to oil or coal or iron and steel. Indeed, the distances with which astronomers must deal are quite beyond the power of our minds to grasp or understand; we can speak of stars as being trillions of miles away from us, but our poor little minds cannot grasp the idea of such distances; we cannot understand what it means,—we can only wonder. We would realize more fully—or, at least, to a slight degree, I will say—the vastness of space, and the distances of these worlds, the stars, from us, should we, first viewing them with our unaided eyes, immediately view them through a number of great telescopes, each of greater power than the one before it. From the 5,000 or 6,000 which those of us with good eyes could see, at the outset, the number would increase rapidly, as each telescope by its greater power would bring to view yet more distant ones, until we should be astounded at their number. And yet, there are others, countless numbers, it may be, still out of reach of even the most powerful telescope yet made; what appear to be but fleecy clouds, as viewed through even powerful telescopes prove, by the use of yet more powerful telescopes, to be stars in numbers almost beyond belief; and with instruments better yet than those we now have, we may expect ever increasing reason for wonder! And marvelous to add, for each star thus seen there are probably many more, close to it, which cannot be seen. Astronomers tell us that each of these far distant bodies—millions of them—must be a sun like our sun, and probably has revolving around it a number of worlds like our own, but which cannot be seen at all. The great universe, then, we are to believe, is made up of countless systems of suns, with their accompanying worlds, similar to our own solar system. Well might the Psalmist exclaim, in wonder: 'What is man, that thou [GOD] art mindful of him?' As for our world, big as we think it is, it is, after all, but a speck in the great universe.

When we attempt to picture all this in our minds—to comprehend the vastness of GOD's great universe—we find ourselves utterly unable to do so, and we are forced to see and realize our own littleness. Nothing, indeed, can give us so exalted an idea of the power and wisdom of GOD,—and of our own littleness, in comparison—as the thought, so far as we are able to entertain it, of the vastness of GOD's creation—of the universe. We are lost, at the very outset, in our attempt to measure space; like eternity, it is without measure or limit, boundless, unending—something beyond our power of thought. When we think, then, of this vastness—space—as fairly swarming with great worlds, not hundreds or thousands, but millions, of them, we can only stand in wonder and amazement at the power of Him who made all these worlds 'in the beginning'; but when we further consider that all these worlds are constantly in motion, flying through space with astonishing speed, the thought of the wonderful power displayed in their creation is almost overshadowed by thoughts of the wisdom which has given to each of these worlds its own place in space, and has so ordered its course and movements that through all the centuries not one has wandered from its path or brought disaster to another! Such power and wisdom are far beyond the conception of human minds. Mitchel, the great American astronomer and geographer, as also gallant soldier, whose studies made him familiar, in a sense, with the wonders of the universe, in speaking of the existence, power and wisdom of God, as contrasted with man's weakness, would illustrate thus: Suppose that even the wisest of men should have placed at his command all these worlds,—or, we may even suppose that he has had power to create them all,—how utterly dismayed and lost would he be, with only his human wisdom to aid him, at even the thought of placing this countless multitude of worlds in space, appointing each its course and setting each in motion so that through all time they should go on unfailingly, unerringly, in perfect harmony, as now they do! Well might he shrink at the very thought of such a task!* Only divine wisdom can direct and control, as only divine power has created, the universe.

Ah, yes, I've been looking for that question, young lady,—what holds up the earth and all these other worlds? That's another of your questions of the more-easily-asked-than-answered kind, I must say. However, it must be answered, in some way, and I'll do my best to help you to understand the matter.—Oh, no, Bess, not like a feather— by the air; that would be impossible. You see, in the first place, the earth is so much heavier than the air that it could not float in it, like a feather; and then, again, the air which, as I told you a moment ago, surrounds the earth in a layer, is really to be considered a part of the earth itself, as it goes with it in its journey through space. If we were to suppose the earth is upheld by the air, we would next have to ask— what upholds the air? and then, again, what upholds this? and so on, without end. Some people, living hundreds of years ago, solved this

---

*"Let a power be delegated to a finite spirit equal to the projection of the most ponderous planet in its orbit, and, from an exhaustless magazine, let this spirit select his grand central orb. Let him with puissant arm locate it in space, and, obedient to his mandate, there let it remain forever fixed. He proceeds to select his planetary globes, which he is now required to marshal in their appropriate order of distance from the sun. Heed well this distribution; for should a single globe be misplaced, the divine harmony is destroyed forever. Let us admit that finite intelligence may at length determine the order of combination: the mighty host is arranged in order. These worlds, like fiery coursers, stand waiting the command to fly. But, mighty spirit, heed well the grand step, ponder well the direction in which thou wilt launch each waiting world; weigh well the mighty impulse soon to be given; for out of the myriads of directions, and the myriads of impulsive forces, there comes but a single combination that will secure the perpetuity of your complex scheme. In vain does the bewildered finite spirit attempt to fathom this mighty depth. In vain does it attempt to resolve the stupendous problem. It turns away, and while endued with omnipotent power exclaims, 'Give to me infinite wisdom, or relieve me from the impossible task!'"—MITCHEL.

puzzling problem of how the world is upheld—solved it to their own satisfaction, at least—by supposing that it rested upon the back of a great turtle,—and they probably did n't trouble themselves with the question Miss Inquisitive would have asked, had she been living then, on what does the turtle rest? But the world is wiser now, and we know that our world is upheld, as are all the worlds of the universe,

THE EARTH IN SPACE.

by GOD who created it and them—by His power alone, as shown in His great law known as the *Law of Gravitation.* Until the existence of this most wonderful law was discovered, by the great English philosopher and astronomer, Sir Isaac Newton, in 1666, the question Miss Inquisitive has asked — what holds up the world?—was an unanswered and an unanswerable one; since this law has become known, however, this question, with other once puzzling ones, can be answered, at least, in a general way.

I will try to explain the matter of this law of gravitation and its workings in the upholding of all the worlds in the universe. The law, in general terms, is this: Each particle of matter in the universe attracts, or draws toward it, every other particle of matter in the universe, with a force in proportion to its mass and its distance. In other words, the smallest particle of anything which helps to make up this world—the finest grain of sand, for instance—attracts, or draws toward it, every other particle, and, on the other hand, every other particle attracts the grain of sand—or whatever else it may be—to it; the grain of sand, then, attracts the whole earth to it, and the whole earth, in turn, attracts the grain of sand. The same is true of all bodies on the earth—rocks, houses, animals, even ourselves. We attract the earth to us, and the earth attracts us to it, but the earth attracts us as much more than we attract it as its mass—or weight, I'll say—is greater than ours. As the earth's mass is so very much greater than our own, you can see that the earth draws us to it with very great force or power. It is this very force with which we are attracted to the earth which keeps us, as also all other objects, upon it—holds us, as it were, fast to it. If this attraction should cease, we would fall or fly off from its surface, through the air, and away off into space. You can understand, then, how important, as well as wonderful, is this law of gravitation. When Ned or Tom, here, tries how high he can throw his ball, it goes up and up, until he feels quite proud of his strength and skill in throwing; but pretty soon the ball stops its upward flight, and in a moment falls back to the ground. He could make a very much higher throw, indeed, if he could cause the law of gravitation to cease to act between the earth and his ball—in which event the ball would never come back. As it is, however, the moment the ball leaves his hand and starts upward, the earth begins to pull it back with a force which soon overcomes the force with which he threw it, and shortly stops it and brings it back again.

Not only are all objects upon the earth thus drawn and held together by this law, but the same law reaches out through all space and takes in all the worlds in the great universe. Our earth constantly attracts all these other worlds, even the most distant, while all of them, in turn, constantly attract the earth; in short, each and every world attracts each and every other world with a force in proportion to the mass and distance of each. In our system—the solar system— the sun is the great center of this attraction, and attracts the earth and all the other bodies belonging to the system with great power; at the same time, the earth and all of these other bodies, attract the sun and each other, but with much less power than that with which the sun attracts them; still further, all these bodies of our system are at the same time attracting, and being attracted by, all the great multitude of worlds throughout the universe, as I have already told you. The result of this attraction of world upon world is to hold each in its proper position in space, as it goes flying along the course appointed for it,—and thus, Miss Inquisitive, our world, with all the others, is upheld. To borrow the illustration of another, we can understand how the earth is upheld in space if we imagine the sun letting down a huge cable, and every star or world in the heavens a cord or thread, to hold the earth in its place, while the earth in return sends back a cord to every one, to help hold them in place. And so we can imagine a cord from each world running to each and every other world, and receiving one from it ; these countless cords, which of course are there only in our imagination, represent the attraction existing between the worlds by reason of the great law of gravitation —a beautiful law, too, you will agree, as well as an important and wonderful one !

But, dear me, how far we have wandered from the matter we had intended to consider ! Let us see if we can find the starting point, again."

IV.

THE SOLAR SYSTEM:—THE PLANETS.

"I had last begun, I believe, to tell you something concerning the solar system, to which our world belongs, and was led away off from that by Miss Inquisitive's big questions ; we will, then, take up this subject, again, and consider it briefly as possible, before we speak of the sun, in particular.

The solar system, then, consists of the *sun*, which is the principal body belonging to it, and is the center of the system ; eight large worlds, or *planets*, as we call them, with the moons which belong to some of them ; a large number of very small planets ; also, *comets*, *meteors* or *shooting stars*, and what is known as the *zodiacal light*. The sun is at the center of the system, our earth and the other planets circling round and round it through space, year after year, being held in their proper courses around it by the very great power with which, on account of its immense size, it attracts them. Of the planets, three are smaller than the earth, while the other four are very much larger. They all are at different distances from the sun, two of them being nearer to it than our earth, and five farther from it. All are round bodies like our earth, and all are constantly in motion around the sun, as I have already stated, and if we could be stationed, as we supposed, awhile ago, a thousand miles or so away from the earth, we should see our big round world, with everything upon it, and the clouds in the air around it, whirling along through space, in this journey around the sun, at what would seem to us a frightful rate of speed—no less, indeed, than 1,100 miles a minute! Aha! I thought that would bring out the 'Oh-h-h's.' Well, you see the earth has a long trip to make in going around the sun —nearly 600,000,000 miles—and it has just a year in which to do it, and so

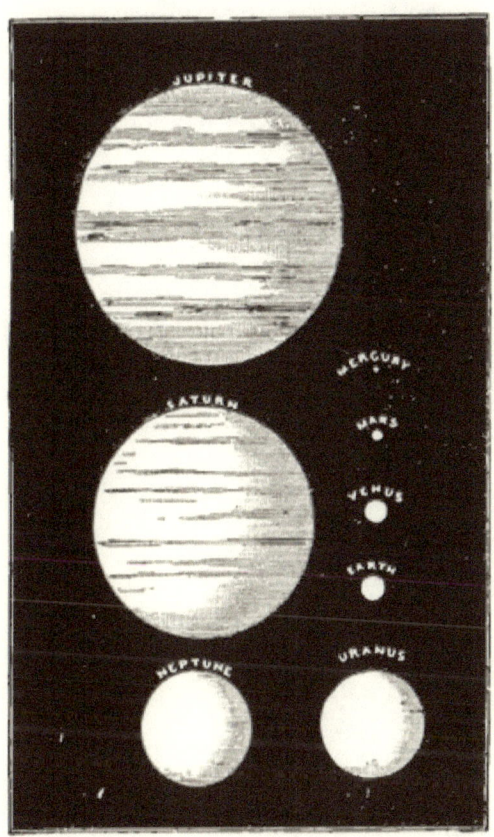

COMPARATIVE SIZE OF THE PLANETS.

it must keep moving at this rate. It is this complete circuit made by our earth around the sun which makes a year—about 365¼ days, as you know. I have spoken of the earth as going around in a circle, but this is not exactly the fact. The course of the earth in its yearly journey is not a perfect circle, but what is called an *ellipse* or, as I may term it, a circle slightly flattened. Here, I'll draw an ellipse, so you will understand some points of which I want to speak. There it is, you see,—and each of the other planets of our system, as well as our earth, follows a similar course. If I were to draw one here for each, two would go inside of this one I have made as the earth's, and five go outside of it. The sun, I should state, is not just in the center of the ellipse, but a little to one side of it. I'll mark the place where it is—thus; and to finish the matter, I'll show the earth, say, just here. Of course there is no real line or path for the earth or planets in space, but they do, however, go around and around in the same general course, just as if there were actual paths there. Now the

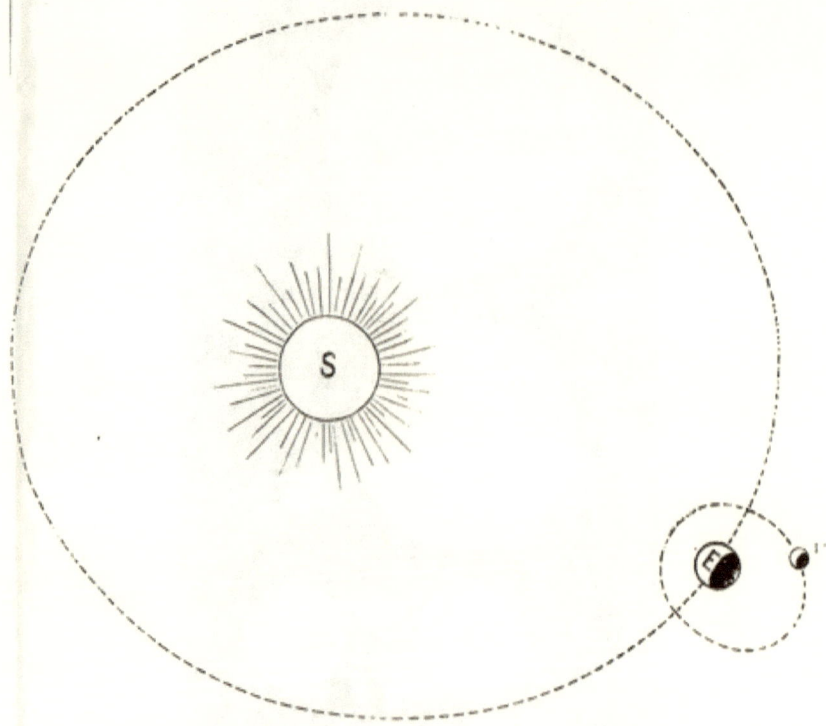

earth's course around the sun—its *orbit*, it is called—is, as I have said, about 600,000,000 miles in extent—a distance too great for us to comprehend, but over which we travel, every year; we may claim to be great travelers, you see, without ever leaving home. You can see that the earth is sometimes farther away from the sun than it is at other times, while making its wonderful journey. Its average distance is about 92,500,000 miles from the sun, but we are about 3,000,000 miles nearer when at the nearest point, here at the left, than when away over here, at the right. When the earth is away out here, moving away from the sun, it moves more slowly, since the attraction of the sun is pulling it back; but after it makes the turn, and starts toward the sun again, its speed increases as the attraction becomes greater until it has made the turn here, again, and again moves from the sun; the average speed, however, is what I told you, a moment ago. Oddly enough, at the time when we are the closest to the sun we are having our coldest weather—our winter; but this seemingly strange condition of things is due to the fact that our part of the earth is not turned so fairly to the sun at that time—for a reason you will learn, some time· ·as it is when we are having our summer. However, the people who live in South America, Africa and Australia are having their summer, at this time, their part of the earth being fairly turned toward the sun, and they receive the benefit of the greater nearness of the sun, their summer being much hotter than ours. I should add that our earth travels in its orbit, as, also, do all the planets from right to left, or in the opposite direction to that of the hands of a clock or watch.

Here, I will make a picture showing the earth in some of its positions in the course of its yearly passage around the sun. Our earth, at this time of the year, is just about where it is shown here at the top of the picture, at December 21st,—that being the date, each year, at which the sun rises and sets farthest south, or, in other words, at which our part of the earth—the part north of the equator—is turned so that it faces the sun the least fairly, and therefore feels his heat the least; this point in our yearly path is called the *winter solstice*, and the date, December 21st, is the beginning of our winter, as counted by astronomers. From this point on, as the earth constantly moves forward, toward the left, along its path, our part of the earth is brought day after day, and week after week, to face the sun more fairly. On December 31st—ten days later than the point of winter solstice—the earth reaches the point in her path at which it is actually closest to the sun, or in *perihelion*, as it is called, a point from which it is just now but about four days distant, as you can see.

As the earth passes on along its course through January and February and into March, we continue to face the sun more fairly, day after day, as I have said, and on March 21st or 22d—the exact time varying slightly, year after year—it will have reached the point at which the sun shines directly upon the equator, and to an equal distance north and south of it, this being the date of the *spring equinox*, or the time when our days and nights are of equal length, and the date, also, when winter ends and spring begins, according to the astronomers. As our earth still moves onward, through April and May and into June, our part of it faces still more fairly toward the sun, day after day, until on June 21st it will have reached the point at which it faces it most fairly during the year. This is the point of the *summer solstice*, and is directly opposite the point of the winter solstice the earth having passed through half a year, and half her path around the sun, since

leaving that point. Spring ends and summer begins with this day—
June 21st—on which date the sun rises and sets farthest north of any
time during the year, making it the longest day of the year, that is,
the day embracing the longest time between sunrise and sunset.

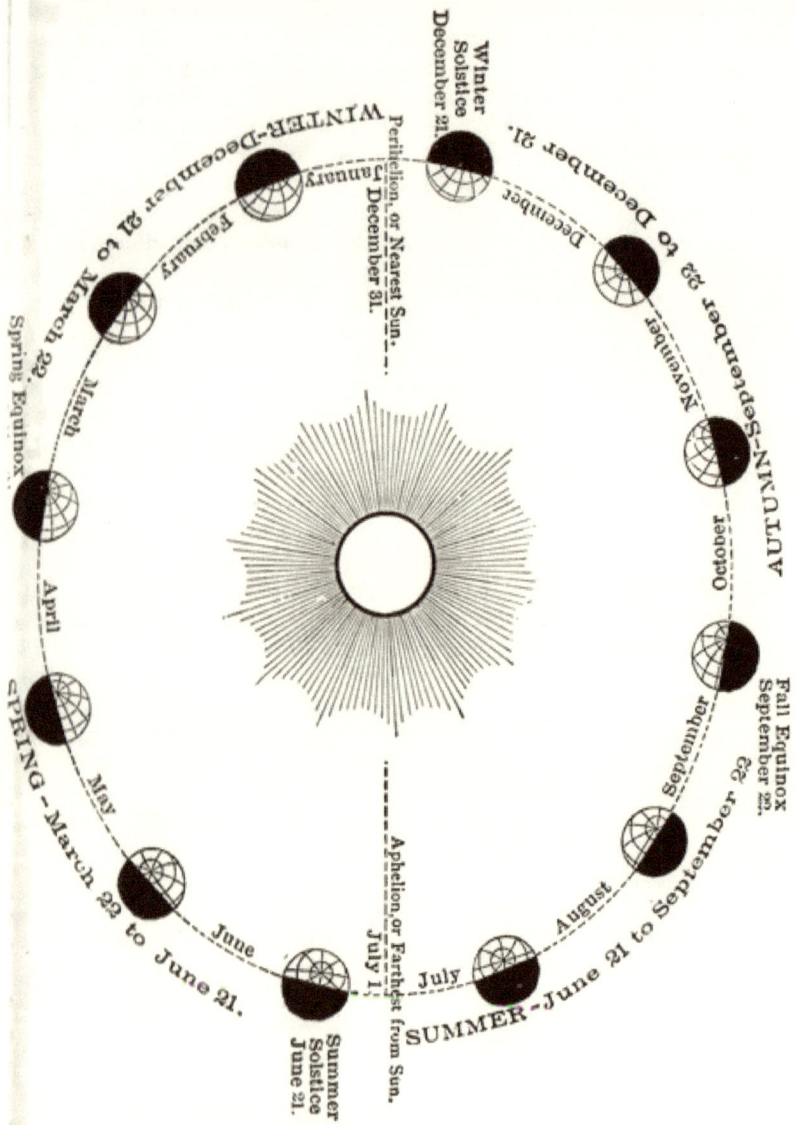

Moving on, we reach, in a few days, the point at which the earth
is farthest from the sun—the *aphelion* point, it is called. As we pass
through the summer months, July and August and into September,

our part of the earth again faces less directly toward the sun, day
after day, and on September 21st or 22d, we reach a point, again,
where the sun is directly over the equator, and shines to an equal distance north and south of it, which gives us, again, days and nights of
equal length; it is the point known as the *fall equinox*—directly opposite from, and six months later than, the spring equinox -and is the
date of the close of summer and the beginning of fall or autumn.

Still moving on through October and November and into December, our part of the earth faces less and less fairly toward the sun,
day after day, so that we feel its heat less and find the cold of winter
again coming upon us, until on December 21st, again, our earth is back
to the point of the winter solstice, where autumn ends and the winter
season begins, having been one year, or about 365¼ days, in thus making the circuit of the sun.

While we have winter, people south of the equator have summer,
and so on through all the year, our seasons and theirs are exactly opposite—all these changes of seasons being due, as I have already told
you, to the fact that the axis of the earth is so inclined, or tilted, toward
its path around the sun, that each part of the earth is made to face
the great, hot sun more or less fairly at different times. You may understand this change of position better, perhaps, by noticing, in the picture, how the north pole, in the winter, is turned away from the sun—
how, as the earth moves on around the sun, it is, after awhile, brought
to face toward the sun, during the spring and summer months and how,
as the earth moves on along the other side of its course, it is made to
face away from the sun, again, during the fall and winter months.
But of this matter of the change of the seasons you will learn more
when you are older.

But besides moving thus around the sun, yearly, the earth, as
some of you may already know, is all the time turning round and
round on its axis, as it is termed, as it flies onward. It turns once
thus every day, or 24 hours, making 365¼ such turns—or revolutions,
we should say—in the course of its yearly journey around the sun.
It is this turning round and round which gives us day and night—day,
while our side of the earth faces the sun,—night, when we have been
turned farther around, so that we no longer face the sun. The
opposite part of the earth -China and other countries—will be facing
the sun, and having their day, you see, while we are sleeping away
the night. Each of the other planets thus turns on its axis, and so has
day and night, as we do, though differing from ours in length.

The moon, which is quite close to the earth as compared with the
sun, keeps constantly circling around the earth while the earth is
circling around the sun ; but we will talk about the moon, in particular,
at some other time.

But we must not forget the other planets. Besides the earth, there
are seven large ones, as stated, named after the heathen gods and

icients, because of some fancied resemblance be-
it, appearance or size of the planet and some sup-
he heathen god or goddess for whom it was named.
t the sun is called *Mercury.* It is the smallest planet,
out twenty times as large as it is. Its diameter—
—is about 3,000 miles. Its average distance from
,6,000,000 miles. Being thus comparatively near,
is greater, and this increases the speed with which
un, which is at the average rate of about 1,770 miles
wice that of the earth! As its course around the
hould say—is much smaller than the earth's, and
reater, it flies around the sun in about 88 of our
ar is much shorter than ours; indeed it has more
rs inside one of ours. Its day, however, is about
is ours, being about 24 hours and 5 minutes.

ius—which some of you may have had pointed out
bright and very beautiful 'morning,' or 'evening
size almost equal to the earth, being about 7,700
The average distance of Venus from the sun is
les. She travels more slowly than Mercury, but
he earth, the rate of speed being about 1,300 miles
ves around the sun in 225 of our days—the length
being considerably more than half one of ours.
lanet in point of size. Her day is about 23 hours
ength.

rom the sun comes our own world, the earth, about
ady given you some of the principal facts and
is fifth in size.

d us comes, next, *Mars*—a planet much smaller
eing but about 4,250 miles in diameter, or next
ury. Its average distance from the sun is about
Being so much farther away from the sun than the
s attraction being less powerful, it moves around in
vly—about 900 miles a minute—and having, as you
reater distance to travel, it requires 687 of our days
d the sun—its year, therefore, being nearly as long
ars has two moons, one of which is but 4,000 miles
e other, a little more than 12,000 miles. One is but
ther about 7½, miles in diameter, being very small,
lve about the planet as our moon does about the
ours, 37 minutes and 23 seconds is the length of

the little planets mentioned. They occupy the
in which we might expect to find another large
ey are supposed, by some persons, to be parts of
t, although others do not believe they ever have

belonged to one large world, but were formed, each as we now find it. Over a hundred of them have been discovered, while it is thought there may be many thousands of them, altogether. They are very, very small worlds indeed, most of them, the largest being but 400 miles in diameter. They revolve around the sun, each in its own orbit, like the large planets, occupying a belt in space about 100,000,000 miles in width, the center of which is distant about 250,000,000 miles from the sun. The number of these little worlds—*asteroids*, they are called—discovered up to September 1, 1889, is 287; new ones are being discovered, every little while, so that it is not yet known how many there are of them. Some are no more than 20 miles in diameter.

Next comes *Jupiter*—the giant planet. Its diameter is about 86,000 miles. It is larger than all the other planets of our system put

SATURN AND RINGS.

together; indeed, it would take about 1,285 worlds like our earth to equal it in size! Its average distance from the sun is 484,000,000 miles, and so great is the distance to be traveled in its course around the sun that although flying along at the rate of 480 miles a minute, it requires about 12 of our years for this planet to make this journey— one of Jupiter's years being, therefore, equal to about 12 of ours. Jupiter has four moons, which go round and round the planet while it goes round the sun. These moons are of considerable size. Jupiter's day is 9 hours, 55 minutes and 20 seconds in length.

Saturn is the name of the next planet we find in passing outward from the sun. Saturn is second in size, among the planets, being about 71,000 miles in diameter. Its average distance from the sun is

886,000,000 miles, and although it travels along its orbit 350 miles a minute its year, or the time occupied in passing around the sun, is equal to over 29½ of our years. Some of you would not be much more than a quarter of a year old, measuring by Saturn's year, eh? Saturn is twice as well supplied with moons, as is Jupiter, having eight of them, which revolve around the planet as do Jupiter's and our own. Besides, Saturn has three great, wide, shining belts or rings which surround it, but at great distances from it, and which also revolve about it. The nature of these rings has not been clearly determined as yet. Saturn alone has such rings; at least, none have yet been found, elsewhere. This planet, with its rings, presents a magnificent spectacle. Saturn's day is but about 10 hours and 14 minutes long.

Uranus, the next planet, has a diameter of about 33,000 miles, it being fourth in size among the planets. Its average distance from the sun is about 1,780,000,000 miles!—figures are growing large, are n't they? So great is the distance it must travel in passing round the sun, that its year is equal to more than 84 of ours. It travels at the rate of about 240 miles a minute, in its path around the sun. Nearly all our earth's inhabitants, counted by Uranus' time, would die before they could reach the age of a single year! Four moons circle around this planet. The length of Uranus' day is not yet known.

Next, and last, we come to *Neptune*, far, far out in space, being distant from the sun an average distance of about 2,800,000,000 miles! It, of course, has an immense distance to travel in its passage around the sun. So great is this distance that it requires nearly 165 of our years to traverse it, and complete one of its years, although it is moving at the rate of 200 miles a minute all the time. Neptune is the third planet in point of size, being 37,000 miles in diameter. Like our earth, Neptune has but a single moon. The length of Neptune's day is unknown.

We have now taken a brief glance at each of the planets. The same law governs them all, although affecting them in different measure, according to their mass and their distance from the great center of the system, the sun. The quantity of heat and light received by each differs very much, of course. On Mercury, the closest, it is several times as great as that which we receive, the quantity then diminishing with each until at Neptune, the farthest, it is but a thousandth part of what our earth receives. Ah, yes, a question I was looking for—but one which cannot be answered, young lady, as you would like it to be. Whether anybody lives on these other planets, or not, no one can say, as not even the best telescopes yet made, or any ever likely to be made, can enable us to settle this point. Only He who made them knows. We know no reason, though, why our world alone should be peopled—filled with life in countless forms; for all we know, or do not know, these other worlds, as all those in the universe, may also be swarming with life.

I should say that the planets, some of which we can see shining among the stars, have no light of their own, but the light which we see coming from them—which makes them shine—is received by them from the sun, and is reflected, or thrown back, to us, just as it is reflected from objects here on the earth. Indeed, our earth which, we know, is not bright, as the stars seem to us, reflects the light of the sun to the other planets, as they do to us; so that if we were on Venus, for instance, the earth would appear to us as Venus appears to us from the earth—shining like a star. Our moonlight, I may add, is sunlight reflected to us from the moon—but of this and other things concerning the moon we are to talk, later.

Now, if I had a sheet of paper large enough, we would soon have a picture showing all the planets circling around the sun—like this little one here which shows the sun and earth only; but to show them all, each at the proper distance to correspond with their real distances from the sun would require a much larger piece of paper than any we have here. For instance, if we should represent Mercury, the planet nearest the sun, as being distant but a little more than an inch from it, Neptune would have to be represented as being about 6½ feet from the sun; and to draw a circle or, ellipse, rather, representing its entire course, or orbit, would require a sheet of paper over 13 feet square. Why, yes, Ned, to be sure we could; that's a very bright idea. Move back your chairs and stools, then, and we'll mark off the distances of the planets on the carpet. You sit still, Miss Inquisitive, I want you to be the sun; perhaps Joe ought to have that position, however—he is so remarkably bright, you know. Now, Willie, bring me your marbles, that rubber ball Bess gave you yesterday, some of baby's little beads, and—let's see—oh, yes! the papers of flower seeds which mamma saved in the fall; with such an assortment of round things, I think we shall be able to find enough of suitable sizes to represent the different planets.

Miss Inquisitive, we'll move your chair just a little this way—that will do—to bring you to the center of the room; now, you are supposed to be the sun, in the center of our solar system. However, we are all to try our best to imagine you as being, not a rather handsome—though modest—young lady, but some kind of a big ball, a foot-ball, say, about a foot in diameter; we will have to represent the sun as being of that size, in order to find enough small round bodies to represent the planets. Ah, here's Willie with our planets, now; that's good—thank you.

Now, we will begin. If we were in a large hall, I would work on a larger scale, but we cannot inside this room place the first planet, Mercury, more than about an inch from the sun without entirely crowding out Neptune, and perhaps Uranus and Saturn. So we will place Mercury here, an inch from Miss Inquisitive—our sun. As she is supposed to be a ball a foot in diameter, Mercury in proportion will be very small, being only 3,000 miles in diameter, you will recollect, while the sun is 870,000,000 miles in diameter!—a fact which I had no yet stated. We will use one of these little pansy seeds to represent Mercury, then, placing it here—this distance of an inch representing the 36,000,000 miles between the planet and the sun. For Venus we will use, as giving us about the proper size, in proportion to our supposed sun, this small sweet-pea, placing it here, about 2 inches from the sun. Our earth comes next, and will, being a little larger than Venus, you know, need, say, this slightly larger sweet-pea, placed nearly 3 inches from the sun. Near it, here, we will place this tiny seed, to represent our moon, you know. Mars, now, will be here, about 4 inches out, and may be represented by this balsam seed. Here, close beside it, I'll place these two tiny seeds for its two moons. The little planets come next, and might, if we had it, be represented by sprinkling here some grains of the finest sand. Next comes big Jupiter—here, about 13½ inches out; the new gum ball, Willie, will just suit for this planet, being about an inch and a quarter in diameter. Here around it we will place 4 little seeds, representing Jupiter's moons. Saturn will be about 24½ inches out—here—and this big marble, a little over an inch in diameter, will fairly represent it. Here, too, are 8 little seeds, for its moons. Out here, about 49½ inches, we will place Uranus, this smaller half-inch marble being about the size to properly represent it. These 4 little seeds represent its moons. And, lastly, away out here, about 78 inches, or 6½ feet, from the sun we will place this marble, which is a little larger than this one for Uranus, to represent far-away Neptune—with this little seed, again, for its moon. There—we have the planets all placed. Now, if we could start them all going, around and around Miss Inquisitive—Mercury fairly flying around and the others traveling each more slowly than the other, in their order from the sun, we could understand more clearly their motion. However, they do not move around as they would here on the floor, all on the same level; indeed, not one of them revolves on such a level, as I may put it. The paths or orbits of all of them are inclined—or 'tipped,' you know —some more, some less, so that their actual paths, as we would see if we could have our planets here move like the real planets, would be partly above and partly below the floor, in what we would call a leaning position, some leaning more, others less. Of course, there is no real thing in space corresponding to our floor here, but astronomers imagine such a thing as existing, and as passing through the center of the sun; this they call the *ecliptic.* As the planets circle round the sun, they will be sometimes above, sometimes below this ecliptic—as we have seen they would be above or below the floor— crossing it twice in each revolution, or year. This is the 'crossing the line' of which you may have heard older persons speak. Our earth 'crosses the line' March 21st, and September 22d, each year;

this time of crossing is called the *equinox*—which means equal night —the days and nights at these dates being of equal length, 12 hours each. But of these and many other things of which I cannot tell you now, you will learn, I trust, when you are older. Astronomy is a beautiful, a wonderful science, as even the little you have learned may have already led you to believe; everybody who can do so, ought to study it, and those who cannot, whether old or young, ought to, if possible, at least read one or more of the many books upon it.

If our room were but large enough, or if we were out on the lawn, I might arrange you, each to represent a planet, and have you all move around Miss Inquisitive, as the sun, Mercury running, or walking very rapidly, and Neptune plodding around very slowly. Some of you, too, could circle around the planets, to represent moons, and others of you might play comet and rush in between the planets, turning round the sun and then rushing out again in real comet fashion. We may try this, next summer; it would be quite a novel lawn game, wouldn't it?—quite as interesting as, and more instructive than, 'fox and geese.'

Comets?—Miss Inquisitive; well, I'll tell you something about them, in a moment, ma'am, as, before speaking of the sun and moon, in particular, we will take a brief glance at the other bodies belonging to the solar system,—a very brief glance, indeed, being all we can catch of some of these bodies, ordinarily, I may add. You all have seen 'shooting' or 'falling stars,' as we call them; probably some of you have seen meteors; while possibly some of you have even seen a comet.—Ah, yes, you have, Ned,—and you, Nell."

V

THE SOLAR SYSTEM :—COMETS, SHOOTING STARS, METEORS AND THE ZODIACAL LIGHT.

"Comets are bright—*luminous* is the proper word—comets are, then, luminous bodies in some respects like, and in others quite unlike, the shooting stars or meteors. They are both a wonder and a puzzle. They are bodies which sweep through space, rushing in between the planets and turning around the sun, appearing to our sight for perhaps several weeks and then disappearing, to return again, some of them, in a comparatively short time,—3 or 4 years, it may be, or 75 or 100 years,—while others of them will not return again for 2,000 or even 3,000 years, and others still not for more than 100,000 years (122,683

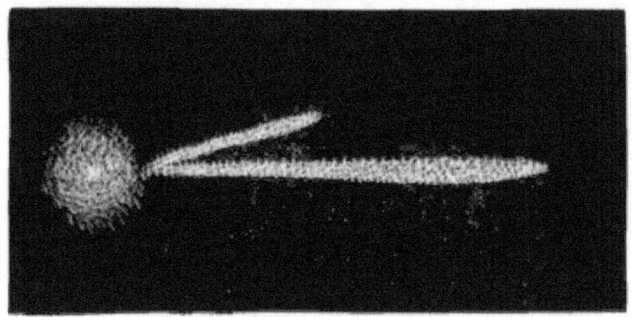

DOUBLE-TAILED COMET.

years in the case of one), so far do their orbits extend out into space! 406,130,000,000 miles—can you think that far, Miss Inquisitive?—is the distance from the sun to which one of them is estimated to travel. The still greater distance to which some others may travel is not yet known.

A perfect comet has a very bright spot called the *nucleus*, surrounded by a less luminous fleecy part called the *coma*, or *envelope*, and this is followed by a long, fleecy tail of light; but some may have no tail; or, they may have several tails—one famous one having been favored with no less than six; or, they may be without a bright central body, or nucleus. Some of them—most of them—move around the sun in the same direction as that of the planets, while others move in the opposite direction. They are first seen as they come toward the sun, though while yet many millions of miles from it. Day by day they draw nearer to the sun, growing brighter all the time, until they swing around it, and fly off again into space—to be gone perhaps a few years, possibly a thousand or many thousands of years. Although traveling swiftly, so great are their orbits that from the time they are first seen until they have doubled around the sun and again gone out of sight is often several weeks—while the astronomers with their great telescopes can see them, too, long before they come within range of our unaided eyes, and long after we can no longer follow them. They can, therefore, be seen night after night, and sometimes even during the day. Usually, when first seen, they are without a tail, only the great, round, fleecy head appearing, with or without a nucleus, as the case may be, the tail appearing, and increasing in length at an astonishing rate, as the comet comes closer to the sun,—this tail generally disappearing as the comet circles round the sun, so that the comet goes off tailless. Sometimes, however, the reverse is true; a comet which starts around the sun without a tail, or with but a small one, develops one at the time when others lose theirs, and goes off with a great tail spreading out behind it! One comet divided, forming two comets, which traveled along, like twins, side by side! This comet was discovered in 1846 by Biela, and received his name. It appeared again in 1852, still separated, but has never since been seen. On this account it is known as the ' Lost Biela.'

Of what comets are composed is not certainly known. The nucleus is probably matter in a more or less fluid state, while the tail is probably composed partly of luminous gas, and partly of countless millions of very, very small bodies, called meteoroids.

Although we see a comet only occasionally, there are, astronomers tell us, millions of them sweeping around the sun. Some of them have appeared many times, coming back to and around the sun every few years, having been familiar visitors for centuries, while others have, as yet, paid us but a single visit.* The time of the return of a comet to our sun, in case it ever returns, depends, of course, mainly upon the extent of its orbit. They do not, I should state, all move in the same kind of orbits; some have orbits like the orbit of the earth, shaped like an ellipse, while others have what are called *parabolic* orbits, and others still, *hyperbolic* orbits. Here—I will make a picture

---

* The following table of periodic comets, in the order of their periodic times, prepared by Prof. Lewis Swift, is the most perfect one extant. There are several other comets whose periods have been computed, but about which there is considerable uncertainty as to their next return.

	Periodic Times.	Next Return.		Periodic Times.	Next Return.
Encke's..........	3.30	1891	Biela's South....	6.63	—
Tempel's I.......	5.20	1889	Wolf's...........	6.75?	1891?
Swift's..........	5.50	1891	Brook's I........	7.00?	1896?
Finlay's.........	5.50?	1892?	Faye's...........	7.41	1896
Brorsen's........	5.56	1889	Brook's II.......	9.00?	1898?
Winnecke's	5.64	1891	Denning's	9.00?	1891?
Tempel's II......	6.00	1891	Tuttle's..........	13.78	1899
D'Arrest's.......	6.39	1890	Pons-Brook's....	71.34	1955
Barnard's	6.50?	1891?	Olbers-Brook's..	72.33	1958
Biela's North...	6.60	—	Halley's..........	76.00	1912

Those marked ? are certainly periodics, but the exact periods are not known, as they have not made another return since they were discovered.

showing these three kinds of orbits. Now, a comet following this inner, or *elliptical* orbit, will at some time come back to the sun, as you can see, but one following this parabolic or this hyperbolic orbit will never come back again to the sun after once swinging round it, for the reason that the sides of its orbit, as you can see, become more widely separated the farther they are extended. In the case of comets following the first named kind of orbit, the time of the return of many of them can be, and has been, determined by the astronomers, who tell us exactly when we may expect to see them again, whether it be in few or many years; but in the case of many of even this kind of comets, so vast are their orbits that it is difficult, if not impossible, indeed, to predict the time of their return. In making the turn round

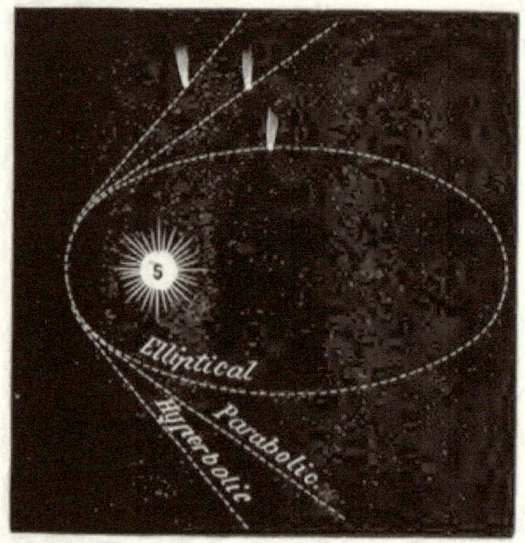

the sun before flying off again, some approach it much more closely than do others. They sometimes come comparatively close to our earth, and the possibility of their striking the earth is talked of; indeed, it is thought the earth did pass through the tail of a comet some years ago, but this is very doubtful.

Some of them are of enormous size—especially in the length and fan-like spread of their tails. Donati's comet—so called because of the name of the astronomer who first saw it—had a tail 50,000,000 miles long. This comet, which probably was seen by the parents of many of you, as it appeared in 1858, was one of the most brilliant and beautiful ever seen. But the comet seen in 1811, though less brilliant than the one just mentioned, greatly exceeded it in size, being 1,125,000 miles in diameter, and having a tail which spread out behind it to a distance of 150,000,000 miles!—while the tail of the comet of 1843 reached the enormous length of nearly 200,000,000 miles, being the longest ever observed. The comet of 1847 (V) was the smallest ever discovered, having a diameter of but 18,000 miles. The nearest approach to the sun made by any comet was that made by the comet of 1843—the one with the remarkably long tail—which, as it turned around the sun, was but 60,000 miles from its surface.

The number of comets discovered, so far as we have reliable records of these events, some of which date back thousands of years, is

DONATI'S COMET.

about 900. During the last twenty years 72 have been discovered. The astronomers of our own country, in the brief time in which observations have been carried on, have already discovered 45 comets. As I have already stated, I believe, there are supposed to be millions of comets, and the discovery of these wandering bodies is a work now receiving especial attention from some of our most noted astronomers, whose great telescopes sweep over the whole sky and pierce to unmeasurable distances the starry depths of space.

Comets, because of the suddenness of their appearance, and their

sometimes seeming terribleness, have always been regarded by superstitious people as messengers or signs of evil—of war, famine, pesti-
lence, etc.—though much less so now than in earlier times, when there
was only ignorance in regard to them.   The comet which appeared in
1861 was thus looked upon by some in connection with our civil war;
but such notions are not very largely accepted in these days in the
light of our present knowledge in regard to comets and their appearances, which are often foretold to a day.   They have always furnished
a most interesting study to astronomers, and still do so, as there is much
yet to learn touching some points concerning them.

The shooting stars and meteors, the astronomers tell us, are small
bodies which revolve about the sun as does our earth.   They
are very, very small bodies, indeed—too small to be seen only as they
flash out when they come so close to the earth as to pass through
our atmosphere—often, too, striking the earth.   The path of the
earth and the path of these tiny bodies around the sun cross
at certain points, and these little bodies that happen to meet the earth
at these points will either pass through our atmosphere and off again,
or strike the earth itself.   They are not bright or fiery, as we see them,
while yet out in space; it is only when they enter our atmosphere that
they become so,—the friction, or rubbing against them of the air, in
their swift flight through it, causing them to glow with heat.   The
very small ones may be entirely burned up, thus, and it is these, or the
bright trail they leave for a moment, that we call shooting stars.
We may see some of these almost any clear night—for it is estimated
that there are hundreds of millions of them.   At some times they are
more numerous than ordinarily, the earth passing across a great belt
of them.   At such times these shooting stars fall by thousands, the air
seeming to be filled with them—much to the terror of the many persons
who do not understand the matter, as thousands do not.   The fathers
and mothers, or grandfathers and grandmothers, of some of you can tell
you startling stories of the wonderful star-shower of 1833.   It was a
most beautiful, although to many, a most terrible, spectacle, indeed.
In 1866 another, though less remarkable shower, occurred, but in England this time.   In ten or eleven years, again, we may have an opportunity to witness one of these great star showers—which occur, as you
will notice by the years I have mentioned, in periods of a little more
than 33 years each, the next being due, therefore, in 1899.   There are
other showers besides that of the 33 year period—one on August 10th
of every year, and others, nearly 200 in all ; but those of the 33
year period are the most remarkable.

There are records of these star showers of the 33 year period dat-
ing back nearly 1,000 years, or to the year 902.   The shower of that
year occurred about the middle of October, but as it occurs one day
later at each return it happens now about the middle of November—
the date of the next one being November 14, 1899.   The cause of these

star showers was a mystery for centuries, but within the last 40 years much light has been thrown upon the matter by the labor of astronomers to that end. It was only with the occurrence of the most remarkable shower of 1833 that it was noticed that the showers occurred at regular periods. It is now known that the countless millions of small bodies which produce these beautiful and startling star showers are collected into rings of millions of miles in extent, in some parts of which they are grouped together more thickly than in other parts. These great rings, or clusters, of *meteoroids*, as the little bodies are called, are (like all the bodies of our system, great or small) revolving around the sun, and it is when our earth, in the course of her yearly journey around the sun, passes through one of these rings or clusters that we have a star shower, the extent of the shower depending upon the number of meteoroids met with in the passage, the number varying with different rings or clusters, or different parts of the same ring or cluster. There are very many of these rings and clusters of these small bodies—one producing the wonderful 33 year shower, another the yearly shower of August 10th, another that of the shower of November 27, occurring every 6 or 7 years, etc., etc.

The 33 year shower is the most remarkable of all. It is produced by a great ring, having in one part of it an immense cluster or swarm of these little bodies. This cluster in the ring is estimated to be 1,000,000 miles in length and 500,000 in breadth and depth, containing millions upon millions of the meteoroids; the other part of the ring is not so large—so thick, we will say. The meteoroids of this ring revolve around the sun once in about 33¼ years. Each year the earth passes through them, but usually through the thinner part of the ring, producing but a small and not at all remarkable shower; but once in 33 years the earth plunges into and through the great cluster in the ring, and we have the shower which startles all who are privileged to behold it,—as perhaps some of us may, in 1899. I have, here, two pictures which will help you to understand this matter of the cause of this great star shower. The first one shows the ring of meteoroids, with the great cluster of them about where it now is, up here. It is coming toward us, and in a little less than ten years from this time, it will have reached us, and on November 15, 1899, we will pass through it. Whether or not we Americans shall be permitted to see the great shower at that time, will depend upon the exact time at which the earth dashes into the stream of little bodies. On the last occasion of this great shower, that is, in 1866, England and the other European countries were so fortunate as to witness it, while we missed it, this being due to the fact that England was facing the stream of meteoroids at the time the earth entered it, and the stream was passed through before the turning of the earth on its axis had brought our part of the earth around to the position which, had it been reached some hours earlier, would have enabled us to witness the shower.

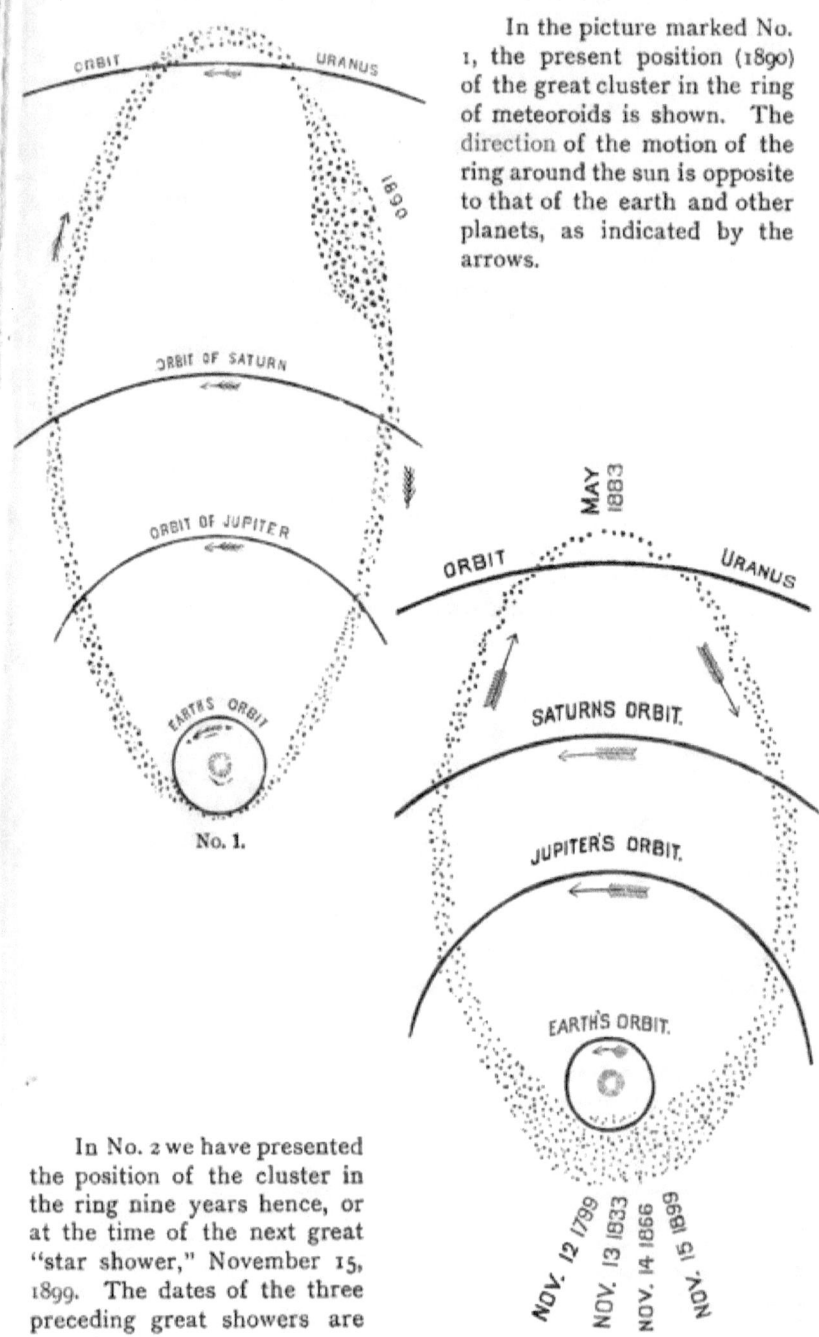

In the picture marked No. 1, the present position (1890) of the great cluster in the ring of meteoroids is shown. The direction of the motion of the ring around the sun is opposite to that of the earth and other planets, as indicated by the arrows.

No. 1.

In No. 2 we have presented the position of the cluster in the ring nine years hence, or at the time of the next great "star shower," November 15, 1899. The dates of the three preceding great showers are also given.

No. 2.

But in 1833 matters were exactly the other way, the eastern continent having been turned on over past the position which would have brought it into the stream of meteoroids had it been reached a little earlier, while our part of the world was brought round exactly in time to face the rain of fire occasioned by the rushing through our atmosphere of countless millions of these little bodies, each of them, as it was burned up by the heat caused by the friction of the air against it, flashing out for an instant and then disappearing in a long, sparkling trail of light.

This shower, judging by the many accounts of it that I have heard and read, must have been a most sublime and beautiful spectacle to anyone not overcome by a feeling of terror—as were perhaps the greater number of those who witnessed it. And such a sight might well strike terror to the hearts of those unacquainted with the nature of such a display, and lead them to believe, as thousands did, that the end of the world had come. The whole sky was filled with the fiery, darting meteors, almost as thickly as with rain, according to some accounts, and continuing for 'eight long, terrible hours,' as one observer says. The same writer says: 'The scene was a most appalling one, and caused the stoutest hearts to quake with fear, and suggested the destruction of the universe.' To the more ignorant and the superstitious the scene was especially terrifying. Its effect upon a large class of such persons is illustrated in the following account given by a South Carolina gentleman:—'I was suddenly awakened by the most distressing cries that ever fell on my ears. Shrieks of horror and cries for mercy I could hear from most of the negroes of three plantations, amounting in all to 600 or 800 souls. While earnestly listening for the cause I heard a faint voice near the door calling my name. I arose, and taking my sword, stood at the door. At this moment I heard the same voice still beseeching me to rise, and saying, "Oh, my GOD! the world is on fire!" I then opened the door, and it is difficult to say which excited me most, the awfulness of the scene or the distressed cries of the negroes. Upwards of a hundred lay prostrated on the ground, some speechless and some uttering the bitterest cries, but most with their hands raised, imploring GOD to save the world and them. The scene was truly awful, for never did rain fall much thicker than the meteors fell toward the earth. East, west, north, south, it was the same!'

This most wonderful of all star showers extended from Greenland to Southern Mexico, and through 40 degrees of longitude. It began before midnight and continued until the brightness of the rising sun hid the meteors from view. Moving at the rate of 65,500 miles an hour, the earth during the eight hours the meteors were visible, passed through 524,000 miles of the great cluster of the ring of meteoroids. As it was estimated that 300,000 of them were seen from any one point, the total number of the meteors or shooting stars which appeared throughout the whole extent of the territory covered by the shower must have been enormous, indeed. Most of them showed the soft white light which we usually see them give, but some were colored— red, green, etc. No doubt the shower of 1899 will be most eagerly watched for,—but its appearance will not be likely to create such widespread fear and alarm as did the shower of 1833.

The source of these myriads of little bodies forming the great rings and clusters is a subject affording food for greatest wonder. It is believed, and with the best of reason, too, that these rings and clusters of meteoroids are made up of the tails of comets, separated from and left behind by the comets in their flight, each return of a comet thus adding to the dimensions of the ring or cluster it has formed, and increasing the number of meteoroids it contains. The proof of this, found by comparing various points connected with comets with the corresponding points connected with the meteoric rings they are supposed to have formed by the repeated loss of their tails, is most conclusive. For instance, the ring producing the great showers of which we have been speaking, is believed to be composed of the cast-off tails of the comet known as Tempel's, the various points connected with the position and movements of the comet and the ring being almost identical.* That 'wonders never cease' is a saying the astronomer is most willing to accept and proclaim, finding, as he does, so many fresh proofs of it on every hand.

I have no doubt it is a matter of surprise to you to learn that the shooting stars are not stars at all, but only the little bodies which are parts of our system,—the real stars being the far, far away suns of which I have already spoken, and of which I may tell you a little more, at another time. The little bodies which are the real shooting stars swarm about us in space all the time, and our earth meets great numbers of them every day, as many as 7,500,000, it is estimated. On any clear night, as you know, we may see some of them, one or more, as they dash into our atmosphere, are heated so as to blaze out for a moment, then disappear forever, having been burned up, to fall to the earth, unnoticed, as dust or ashes. As they never reach the earth only as thus burned to dust or ashes, their real size, shape and appearance is not known, but they are too small, at least, to be seen only as they flash out at night on entering our atmosphere, at the rate of perhaps nearly 100 miles a second ! It is estimated that they flash

---

*The following table of comparisons (Swift) exhibits the striking similarity mentioned:

	Tempel's Comet.	November Meteors.
Period	33.18 years	33.25 years
Eccentricity	0.9054	0.9046
Perihelion Distance	0.9765	0.9873
Semi Axis, Major	10.324	10.344
Inclination	17° 18′	17° 44′
Longitude of Node	231° 26′	231° 28′
Longitude of Perihelion	60° 28′	56° 25′
Motion	Retrograde	Retrograde

out when about 73 miles above the earth, and are burned up, and so disappear, at the height of about 50 miles above us.

Meteors differ from shooting stars in that they are larger, appearing as large balls of fire which may be seen for a considerable time—often during the day time.   Perhaps some of you may have read newspaper accounts of the appearance of meteors in various parts of the

A METEOR WITH ITS TRAIN.

country, or other countries; of how they have struck the earth, and afterwards have been found, hissing and glowing hot, half buried in the earth; and, it may be, they have exploded, with a tremendous report, either while in the air or after having struck the earth.   They are probably the larger of the tiny bodies, which are not, therefore, in all cases, burned up in their passage through the air, and so reach the earth—the explosion, when it occurs, being the result, however, of the heat caused by their passage. The parts of these bodies which fall to the earth are often called *aerolites*. They are largely composed of iron—the *meteoric iron* of which I told you, I think, last year when we were learning some things about iron and steel; some, however, are composed, mainly, of stone.

There is yet the zodiacal light of which I should speak. This is

ZODIACAL LIGHT.

something of which little, if anything at all, indeed, is known beyond the fact of its appearance. It is a great field of light, appearing before the morning twilight or after the evening twilight, having a broad base at the horizon, sloping to a rather rounded top, which top is often high up in the sky. In countries lying at or near the equator, it can be seen every clear morning or evening, being quite bright. Here in the north it is to be seen, when seen at all, only in the early spring, when it appears in the evening, as the stars are beginning to 'come out,' or in the early autumn, when it appears in the morning twilight. It is now believed to be a great ring of matter in the form of dust or of very, very small particles, probably thrown off by comets. It is supposed to be distant about 200,000,000 miles from the sun.

Speaking of the stars as 'coming out' in the evening suggests a point which I think I should mention. As the stars—those far away suns—are everywhere present throughout space, the sky is full of them by day as well as by night, the reason we cannot see them being, the greater brightness of the sun swallows up their light, as it were; and it is only when the light of the sun fades away, as our part of the earth turns away from it, in the evening, that the stars can be seen, the brighter ones coming out first, and the fainter ones as the darkness increases. An astronomer can see the stars by daylight, however, as readily as at night, as the long tube of his telescope shuts out, very largely, the light of the sun. Perhaps some of you may have heard—I have—a well-digger speak of seeing stars when looking up from the bottom of a deep well—the well shutting out the sunlight, as does the astronomer's long telescope.

Now, we must close our talk, for this evening, as I know of several Sunday-school Christmas-trees in which some of you are very much interested, I think; besides, the sick girl may be getting tired.—Oh! you're not tired, eh? Very well, then—we'll go before you are. So, good-by, ma'am, until to-morrow evening; we'll come again, then, at, say, seven o'clock, at which time we will take up the subject we tried to take up at the outset—the sun. Come, youngsters, we'll be off. Good night!—good night!"

VI

THE SUN:—AN EXCURSION TO IT.

"Well, here we are again,—and none of us much the worse, so far as I can discover, for our Christmas feasting. You all had a fine time at your treats, last night, I suppose.—Yes, indeed, to be sure you had—why should n't you? Miss Inquisitive, do they expect you to eat all these good things they have saved from their shares of the treats and brought to you? If so, old Doctor Pillsbury will be needed more than he has been at any time yet, in your case. Come, come, Joe,—at it again, are you? This may, indeed, be a striking illustration of 'sweet friendship,' as you say, young man, but you are on the high road to meeting with a striking illustration of the opposite sentiment, if you persist in presenting such jokes to this company. But I'm afraid my warning is lost on you—judging by that grin; I should n't wonder if you are thinking up something else of the kind, this minute.

Well, mount your throne, Miss Inquisitive, and the rest of you gather around to suit yourselves—only be kind enough to leave empty a certain big chair for a certain big friend of yours to fill, when he can get to it. Thank you—this is comfortable, indeed. Now, if Joe will assure us that he has subsided for the present, we'll begin our astronomical talks again.—Very well, young man, we'll see if you have.

We are to talk about the sun, this evening, I believe—that great body from which we get our heat and light, and which, as you have already been told, is the center of our system around which all the planets, etc., constantly revolve, and by the attraction of which they are held in place while thus flying through space. Considering the fact that the sun is the principal body belonging to our system, controlling all the others, it would seem that we should have given our attention to it before describing the planets as we have done ; but we were led to follow the course we have taken by the questions asked, only reaching the sun, now, after having, in a sense, for a long time been circling around it—or around *him*, I might have said, since the sun is very generally spoken of as being of the masculine gender, the moon, on the other hand, being considered as being feminine, notwithstanding the fact, in this latter case, that we never hear of the woman but only of the '*man* in the moon.'—No, not now, Miss ; we'll talk about that gentleman, again,—to-morrow night, perhaps. But to return to the point of which I was speaking, I will add that I am not

sorry that we are only now about to speak of the sun, as the knowledge thus already gained in regard to some matters, may help you
to more readily understand some of the other matters of which I shall
speak, presently.

I have already told you of the sun's distance from our earth,
about 92,500,000 miles, as you will recollect,—a distance not nearly
so great as others of which I have spoken, yet one of which it is
entirely beyond the power of our mind to form any idea. To enable
our mind to grasp such figures, in a manner, the plan is generally
adopted, by those who speak or write of this and other distances in
space, to apply some familiar rate of speed, as that of railroad trains,
to the measurement of the distances which otherwise defy our powers
of thought. We can realize more forcibly the necessity of some such
illustration when we consider that while nearly anybody can think
pretty accurately touching the distance of a mile or of several miles,
perhaps, yet when we speak of several hundreds, or at most of several
thousands, of miles, only a few can measure even such distances in
their mind; how utterly must we fail, then, in the attempt to *think*
millions of miles. We will, of necessity, make use of such an illustration, going on an imaginary excursion to the sun ; and since we will
take first-class, unlimited tickets, we will then be entitled to ' stop-off
checks,' in case we should care to stay a short time at any planets we
might happen to meet.

We will suppose, then—for we can, at least, suppose all such impossible things as this—we will suppose that there is a railroad
running from our earth away out through space to the sun. What a
long line that would be, indeed ; and oh, how the great, rival ' railroad kings,' as we call them, who now boast of the thousands of
miles of railroad they control here in the United States, would scheme
and plan and work, day and night, to buy up enough shares of the
company owning this railroad to secure control of this line of over
92,500,000 miles ! Well, we will suppose that we take a train upon such
a railroad—a modern vestibule train of parlor, dining and sleeping
cars, it is quite necessary to suppose we have the dining and sleeping
cars, you 'll find, and even more important to suppose we have a very
large and very well stocked provision train accompanying us to supply
our dining car. And, most important of all, we must suppose—since
supposing is so easy and withal so necessary in this case—we must
suppose, before starting upon our trip, that we are to be gifted with
very, very long lives, as, otherwise, we never should reach our journey's
end.—Oh, you 'll soon find out why, Miss Inquisitive—just wait.

Let us suppose, next, having got aboard our train, that we are
running toward the sun at—well, what rate ?—a mile a minute ? No,
that's faster than trains run, except on rare occasions and for but a
short distance at a time, but we 'll say at the rate of 40 miles an
hour, which is the rate at which some of our fast express trains go

rushing across our country, every day. We are now speeding along, we must suppose, at the rate of 40 miles an hour, or 960 miles a day—a rapid rate for railroading, to be sure, but no better than a snail's pace, as compared with the rate at which our world, as we have learned, is rushing along through space around the sun, traveling farther in a single minute than our express train travels in a whole day !

* * * * * * * * * * * * *

Eh ?—what's the matter ? Why, I was just dropping into a comfortable little nap, feeling rather drowsy, as a result, I suppose, of yesterday's over-excitement. There will be plenty of time—plenty of time, indeed—to finish our talk before we reach the sun, and so I have concluded to take a short nap. Please wake me up, some of you, before we reach the moon.—Oh, yes—to be sure, to be sure ! we're only *supposing* that we are on our way to the sun; well, I'll wake up, then, and get to work, again.

Still supposing, then, that we could take a train for the sun, and should travel at express train speed of 40 miles an hour—960 miles a day—let us see how long we would be in making the trip. Let us suppose, too, that we take with us on our train every man, woman and child in the United States—60,000,000 people, we'll say.—Why, Miss Inquisitive, I want to use them as mile-posts, if we may call a person a post, dropping off a man or a woman, or a boy or a girl, at each mile as we speed along. Yes, a rather odd idea, I'll confess ; but you'll understand after awhile, why we are to suppose this. Now, at 40 miles an hour, day and night, and never stopping for a single second, how long, do you guess, would it be before we should reach the moon ?—supposing the moon should happen to be directly on our course at the proper time for us to meet it, being thus directly between the earth and the sun, as it occasionally is, as you will learn, later. No—no—no—all wrong ; but I didn't expect anything else, however, since you were guessing entirely in the dark, as it were ; I simply wanted a few guesses so as to surprise you the more, perhaps, with the real figures. Here, Ned, you may work out the problem for us. Taking the average distance of the moon from the earth—which distance I had not yet told you—as about 238,000 miles, how long would we be on the way between the earth and the moon, traveling as we have supposed at the rate of 40 miles an hour ? The moon, you see, is really quite close to us, as compared with the other bodies of the solar system and of the great universe, yet it is still a long distance from us. Well, Ned, let's see what you have. Ah, yes, that's correct,—it would require over 8 months of steady day and night traveling to reach the moon. A long trip, you think, eh ? Why, we've hardly got fairly started, as you will soon learn ; yet if we should have dropped off our mile-posts regularly, we should have thus left behind us, already, as many people as we have in some of our fairly large and important cities.

Passing by the moon without stopping,—as we will visit it again, —our train, we will suppose, continues on its way toward the sun, probably meeting with many of the very little bodies of the kind which, passing through the earth's atmosphere, become what we call the glowing meteors or shooting-stars, as I explained, last night. Possibly, too, we might meet, or pass near, a comet or two. But the first important body we might meet would be the planet nearest us, Venus. However we could not meet this planet on this trip, I must state. You know our supposed railroad is a straight one from the earth to the sun, and of course we could only meet Venus in case she should reach the crossing of our railroad with her path around the sun at the same time that we should reach it—the earth, Venus and the sun lying then, you will see, in a straight line with each other. But owing to the difference in the times of revolution of the earth and Venus around the sun, and of the difference in the degree of inclination—or leaning or tipping, as we called it last night—of their orbits or paths, it is only at long periods that these three bodies, the earth, Venus and the sun, happen to come thus in a straight line. At these times we can see Venus passing between us and the sun, looking like a small, round, black spot against the sun's bright face. I told you, you will recollect, that the planets are not bright of themselves, but only appear bright or shining by reflecting the sunshine which falls upon them; when Venus thus passes directly between us and the sun, the side on which the sun is shining is, of course, turned away from us and the planet has her dark side —her back, as it were—turned toward us, and it is for this reason that she appears as a round black spot on the sun. This passage directly between us and the sun, is called the *transit* of Venus, and is an occurrence of much importance to astronomers, as it is by observing this transit with special instruments, from different points on the earth, and then comparing the results of their observations, that the astronomers have learned for us our distance from the sun. I had, I may say, a fine view of the last transit of Venus, as it occurred, where I then was, during a heavy forenoon snow storm which, while it did not hide the sun, so lessened its brightness that it could be looked at steadily, without having one's eyes dazzled in the least. I was thus able to watch the passage across it of the round black spot—Venus—during the whole time of the transit—five or six hours, if I rightly recollect. Although Venus is nearly as large as the earth, as I have told you, it appears, as thus looked at against the sun, as but a small round body, this being on account of its great distance from us. The date of this last transit was December 6, 1882; the last one before this was on December 8, 1874, or 8 years earlier, and the next one will not occur until June 7, 2004, or 121½ years later than this last one of 1882. The transits of Venus occur only in periods as follows:—8 years—121½ years—8 years —105½ years; then 8 years—121½ years, etc., over and over again. As it will be 114½ years until the date of the next transit, it is hardly likely that any of us will get to witness it.

So, we shall have no chance to stop at Venus station as our train speeds on and on toward the sun, since our train and Venus will not be at the crossing point at the same time.   Supposing, however, that we have reached the point at which we should find Venus, if she were here, we will be now over 23,000,000 miles from home, as this is the closest that our earth and Venus ever come to each other; rather far-away neighbors, aren't we?   Supposing we have been dropping off, all along, our living mile-posts our train would now be much less crowded, as the big party with which we set out would be reduced nearly one-half, as you can see.   And how long, do you suppose, will we have been on the way?   Take your pencil, again, Ned, and give us the fig-ures.—Yes, that's correct, although you look as though you were not half sure it is.   Here it is, youngsters:—At 40 miles an hour, or 960 miles a day, we will travel in a year, or 365¼ days, 350,640 miles; and at this rate, to travel to Venus, by the shortest 'air-line route,' will re-quire—what do you think?—nearly 66 years!   Ha, ha! how dreadfully astonished you look; you are ready to believe, now, in the necessity for sleeping and dining cars, and a big provision train, aren't you?

Well, we must keep moving along, as we are yet still less than one-fourth the way to the sun.   Mercury would be the next important body we might meet, if it should be at the place at which we cross its path at the same time we are.   But as in the case of Venus, we shall not reach that point at the proper time to enable us to step off upon the planet to enjoy, by way of change, a little walk; I think we would all be quite willing to spend a day or two in walking should we have such an opportunity to do so, as the nearest the earth and Mercury ever approach each other is about 47,000,000 miles, to cover which dis-tance, even at the rate of 40 miles an hour, would have required—ah! I see you are at it, Ned; that's correct—we would have been on the way for over 134 years!   And now you see the necessity for supposing we have been granted unusually long lives.

Still on and on we go, with no other planets to meet—unless, in-deed, we should happen to find *Vulcan*.   Vulcan is the name given to a *supposed* planet, which is even closer to the sun than is Mercury. Certain astronomers formerly supposed or believed there was such a planet, but it is not now so believed.   It is not at all likely, therefore, that we shall meet, or even see, such a planet.   So we may count upon an uninterrupted run to the sun.   As we are at this time of the year the nearest to the sun, the 31st of December, the last day of the year, being the date, always, when we are the very closest to the sun, or, say, about 91,000,000 miles from it, we should, Ned, be how many years in reaching it, at our unceasing, 40-mile-an-hour rate of traveling?   Very good—you are getting quite familiar with these calculations, Ned. According to Ned's figures, then—and they are correct—our trip from the earth to the sun will occupy about 260 years! or, if we had started on July 1, when we are 3,000,000 miles further from the sun, or about

94,000,000 miles distant, we should be over 268 years in making the trip!—Dear me! I've heard a great many 'Oh-h-h!' choruses from you, but that one certainly was the largest and longest by far. And, yet, youngsters, this great distance which would require so long a period of travel to reach it, is considered as but a small one by the astronomers. Indeed, they use this distance of the sun as a small and convenient measure for the very much greater distances with which they become familiar, speaking of many thousands of times the 'sun's distance' as familiarly as we speak of the few miles' distance between two places.

To go back a little, you will see that when only 60,000,000 miles on our way we would have exhausted our great supply of mile-posts; in other words, the great and boasted population of our whole country, if placed a mile apart, would not reach two-thirds of the distance to the sun, an illustration which may help us to form an idea of such a distance —which, Miss Inquisitive, is the reason I made use of what you termed an odd idea. Further, to supply mile-posts for the whole length of our 'Earth & Sun Air Line Railroad' we should have to borrow and take with us, besides all our own people, about three-fourths of all the people of France, or, of Great Britain and Ireland!"

VII.

THE SUN:—ITS SIZE, CONSTITUTION, ETC.— THE SPOTS, PROTUBERANCES, CORONA, ETC.

"As we should approach the sun, on such a journey, we should find its light and heat becoming stronger and stronger until we should be unable to bear either; indeed, we should probably be thus overcome long before we should have even reached our nearest neighbor Venus. We can see, therefore, that if Venus is inhabited like the earth, the people would, no doubt, differ from us in at least their ability to bear the much greater degree of heat and light which they receive, as naturally as we bear that which we receive, here on the earth; and the same would be true in regard to the people who may live on Mercury, where the heat and light are so very much more intense.

We should find, of course, that the sun would appear larger and larger as we approached it, year by year, until, supposing we were not burned up by the heat, or blinded by the light, we should find it a globe of vast size—one beside which our earth would be but a very, *very* small thing, indeed.

How large? Well, we consider our world a pretty large affair, so large that the most of us never see more than a very small part of it, while we naturally have an extra measure of respect for those persons who have visited foreign lands, and especially for the very few who have been round the world and nearly all over it; but it would take a great many globes like our world to make one the size of the sun—no less than about 1,326,500 of them! Aha! that brings the 'Ohs!' and the 'Mys!' as I expected. I may go further and tell you that, should we put all the planets together—big Jupiter and Saturn

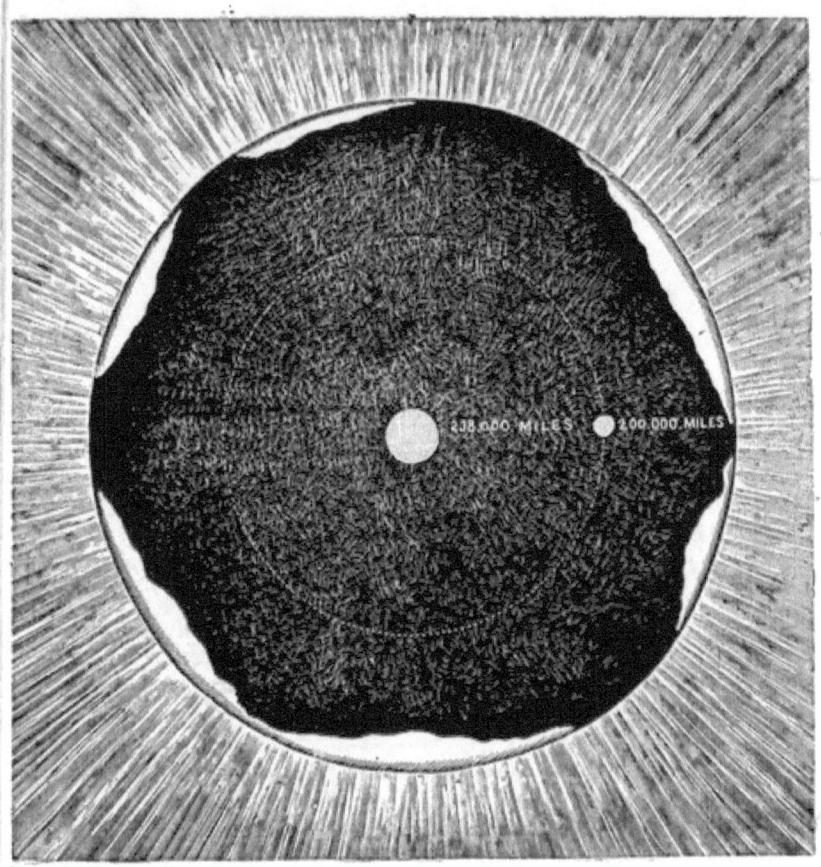

and all the rest,—the sun would be 540 times as large as the whole of them.

Our earth, you know, is nearly 8,000 miles in diameter—about 7,918 miles, to be more exact—while the sun is about 870,000 miles in diameter; so, if the sun were hollow, our earth might be rattled around in it like one of baby's tiny beads in her toy balloon! Indeed, if the earth were at the center of the sun, the moon could circle around it, as it does now, at an average distance of about 238,000 miles, while there would still be a strip or belt about 200,000 miles wide, all around, between the path of the moon and the outside of the sun—as this picture I am drawing will show.

However, the sun is not hollow, but is a solid body as is our earth —only it is much less solid or dense, as we should call it, than the earth, its density being but a little more than one-fourth that of the earth. But, by reason of its great size, the sun's weight is enormous, over 700 times that of all the planets, and other bodies of our system, together. It is this great superiority in weight, or mass, I should say, which enables it to hold the planets all in their courses as they unceasingly revolve around it—all in obedience to the wonderful and beautiful law of gravitation, GOD's law for the control of the great universe He has created!

If we could stand upon the sun and look off into space, we should see the planets looking only like stars circling around us, each in its own path, one lying out in this direction, another in that,—not all on the same level, but some higher, some lower, on account of the inclination or leaning of their paths, of which I have already spoken, some being in the upper, others in the lower part of their paths or orbits. Mercury would be seen fairly flying around, making the circuit of the sun in about 88 of our earth-days, Venus moving less swiftly, and next, our earth, still more slowly, occupying about 365¼ of our earth-days in making her circuit; and so on, each moving less swiftly, until we should see—if it were but possible for us to do so—we should see far-away Neptune, circling around most slowly of all. Each, too, would be turning round and round on its axis, each portion having day as it was turned so as to face the sun, and night as it again turned away from the sun and faced out into space in the opposite direction. We can see why a person, while facing toward the sun, as during the day, cannot, on account of its brightness, see the stars which lie far out beyond the sun in space; and how the stars which lie off in the other direction begin to 'come out' as he is carried around, as the earth revolves, until the sun is hid from him and its light no longer interferes. We can, as you will understand, see the stars only in the part of the heavens opposite to that in which the sun is located,—we look off at night in a direction exactly opposite to that in which we look by day; but as we circle round the sun we are able, in the course of each year, to view the stars in every part of the heavens—just as we can see all the pictures on the walls, here, by turning round so as to face each part of the room in turn.

We have been supposing, now, that we have been comfortably located upon the sun, watching the movements of the earth and other planets around it; but you will readily understand that we would hardly be very comfortable if on the sun, when I tell you that the heat of the sun on its own surface, is estimated to be about 300,000 times as great as we feel it here on our earth!—a degree of heat of which we can form no idea. If we—I declare, young lady, if there is an extra hard question connected with any subject, that's the question, above all others, which is sure to pop into your mind—and out of it, as surely, through your lips. What makes the sun so hot?—a fine question, indeed! one which has long puzzled the wisest heads, and which has not yet been settled beyond dispute. As the heat and light of the sun are constantly being thrown out into space, on all sides of the sun, and have been thus thrown out for untold ages—many millions of years it may be—you can see that its cause or source, whatever it may be, must be constant and inexhaustible. The quantity of heat constantly being sent out from the sun is enormous, that which our earth catches, as it were, or all the planets combined, catch, being but a very small part compared with that which fills the vast expanse of space lying between the planets, on all sides of the sun. Many conjectures, opinions and theories have been offered regarding the source or cause of this enormous volume of heat given off by the sun. Some persons have supposed the sun is burning up, and so burning out, as it would if composed of combustible material like our coal; but this theory is no longer accepted. Others have supposed the heat and light of the sun to be caused by electricity—as we see it in our electric lights; but this theory is not accepted either. Another theory, once pretty generally accepted, is, that the sun by its great power of attraction draws into it vast numbers of meteors and comets, with which it is constantly surrounded, and it is the striking of these bodies against the sun, as they are drawn with tremendous speed and force into it, which produces the heat. I may state—what you will understand better, when older —that the sudden stoppage of motion of any kind changes the motion into heat—something which is constantly occurring around us, every day, but which is not ordinarily noticed; you may prove my statement, however, by hammering rapidly and forcibly upon a piece of iron and then placing your hand upon the head of the hammer. The constant pouring in upon the sun of these meteors, etc.,—or bombardment of it, we may call it, by them—would generate or produce a large amount of heat, no doubt; yet, though this may account for a part of it, it is not now believed to be the principal cause or source of the sun's heat. The opinion—or theory, I should call it—now most fully accepted by astronomers and other scientific men is, that the sun is slowly shrinking, or growing smaller—very slowly, I should add; too slowly to be noticed, even by the watchful astronomers, with their great telescopes —and as a consequence of this shrinking—as you will also understand better, later—the great heat of the sun is produced, aided to some extent, probably, by the falling upon it of the meteors and comets. According to this theory, the sun to the very center of its great mass, is in an intensely heated condition, but is not being burned up as coal is burned up.

I may add that, in support of the belief that the sun's heat and light is due to electricity, we have the statement from Prof. Swift that he noticed, during an eclipse occurring a few years ago, what he considers great lines of electricity streaming off from the sun. But whether or not the sun's heat is due to electricity, it is certain that the sun is the great center of electric force—a fact to which I may refer a little later.

But whatever its source, this we know, that all life on our earth, from that of the tiniest blade of grass to that of man himself, depends upon the heat sent to us by the sun ; without it all would be death— ours would be a dead world ! Remember this, next summer, when tempted to complain about the hot weather.

The degree of heat sent out by the sun is probably pretty nearly the same at all times, the difference which we notice between summer and winter being due, as I have already told you, I believe, to the fact that our part of the earth is turned less fairly toward the sun during our winter months, and the sunshine which brings us the heat falls upon us then in a slanting direction, instead of almost straight down upon us as during our summer months. If the axis of the earth were not inclined—or tilted—toward the earth's path round the sun, giving these changes of position of the different parts of the earth as regards the sun, we would have no change of seasons, but each part of the earth would receive the same degree of heat, and so have the same season, all the year round, forever—a condition of things not to be desired, at all. In this matter, as in everything else in the great universe, we are made to see the wonderful wisdom of the great Creator in always suiting means to the securing of certain necessary ends.

As in regard to the matter of the source of the sun's heat and light there is, or has been, much difference of opinion as to the constitution of the sun—that is as to the elements of which it composed. Without taking up these different opinions or theories, I will give the generally accepted facts in regard to the matter. By the use of an instrument called the *spectroscope*—which I shall not now try to describe or explain to you—it has been ascertained that the sun contains very many of the elements contained by our earth, as iron, zinc, hydrogen, etc. But as the sun's density is only about one-fourth that of our earth, as I have already told you, it is believed that but a comparatively small portion of the sun is of a solid or liquid nature, the greater part of it being of the nature of vapor or gas. Of the solid portion of it, however much or little of it there may be, nothing is positively known, as it is at the center, surrounded and covered up by the gaseous portion ; it is, however, supposed to be in an intensely heated state, as I have already told you. It is believed that there is an atmosphere— very different from ours, however—next to the solid center, in which float layers of clouds at different levels—that is, at different distances from the solid body of the sun, below. The upper part of this atmosphere is intensely hot and intensely luminous, or bright; it is called the *photosphere.* Outside of this again is another atmosphere, or *envelope* as it is termed, of a transparent, gaseous nature—to some extent, perhaps, similar to our own atmosphere.

To the astronomer, aided by his great telescope which appears to bring everything so much nearer, the sun presents very many strange appearances. The whole surface of the sun presents what is described as a mottled appearance, as though it were made up of great, rough points with cavities between them. These points are the brightest

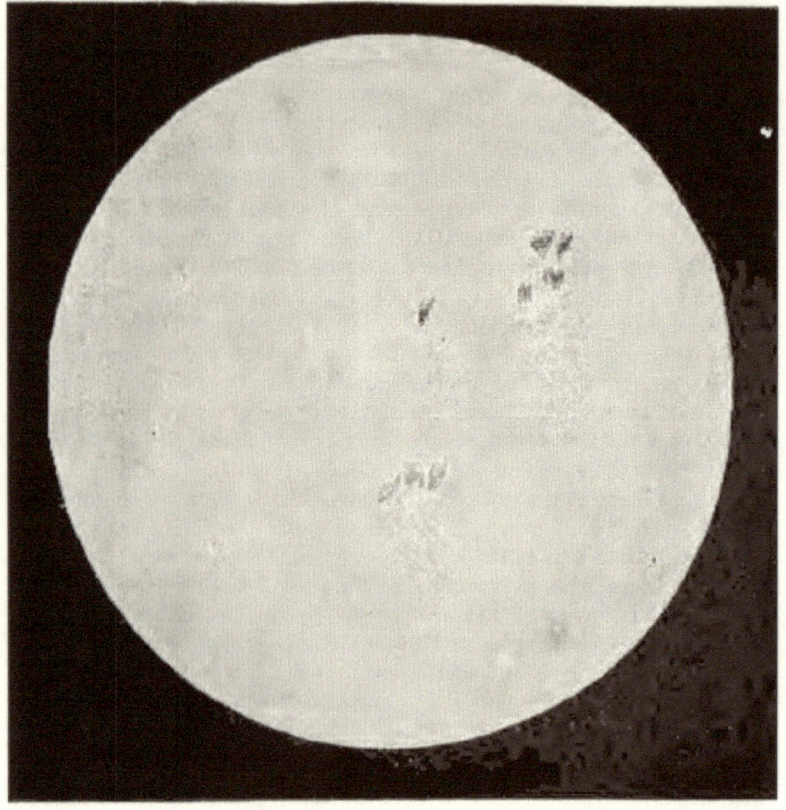

GREAT GROUP OF SUN SPOTS.

The sun, June 18, 1885, photographed by Henry C. Maine.

parts of the sun's surface, which has led some astronomers to believe that it is chiefly from these rough points that the sun's light and heat are radiated, or thrown off into space.

There are frequently seen on the face of the sun great, ragged black spots—perhaps some of you have heard mention made of sun spots. They are irregularly-shaped patches with a black center called the *nucleus*, around which is a border less dark called the *umbra*, and outside of this again a grayish border called the *penumbra*. Sometimes, however, some one of these parts may not be present. These spots vary in size from very small ones to others 50,000 to nearly 200,000 miles in diameter. These large spots may sometimes be seen by the eye alone. I remember to have once watched at intervals, for an hour or two, some very large sun spots, a heavy fog obscuring the sun sufficiently to admit of one's looking at it without being dazzled by the light, as would be the case, ordinarily. I should say, just here, that should you want to look at the sun, at any time when it is shining brightly, use a piece of colored glass, or, still better, smoked glass, through which you may examine it without injury to your eyes.

There has been much speculation in regard to sun spots—their cause, nature, etc. It is generally accepted, however, that they are openings in one or more of the atmospheres surrounding the sun caused, probably, by currents of vapor forcing their way upward and outward from the highly-heated interior; the black central portion of the spot is what may be seen of the solid body of the sun or of one of the interior cloud-layers, as we look down into the opening, the lighter bordering portions being the edges of the overlying atmospheres. Near the spots, too, are commonly seen very bright streaks or ridges; these are called *faculæ*, and are supposed to be the luminous atmosphere, or photosphere, heaped up around the edges of the opening which the rising vapor has made through it. These bright streaks or faculæ are sometimes seen crossing the spots like bridges, dividing them into two or more parts.

The spots move across the face of the sun, about 14 days being required for such passage, reappearing again about 14 days later—when they reappear at all; for, I should state, they are not permanent, but sooner or later disappear; some last for but a very short time—a few hours, perhaps—though others may remain for several weeks or even months, making several trips around the sun. It is the turning of the sun on its axis which causes the spots to thus move forward, the spots not going forward of themselves, but being carried around by the turning of the sun, as we are carried around by the turning of the earth on its axis. It was this movement of the spots which led to the discovery of the fact that the sun does thus turn on its axis, which it does once in about 25⅓ of our days.

The spots are constantly changing in size and shape, though some of them preserve the same form, in general, for a long time. These changes may be due to the continued rushing through the openings in the atmospheres of vapors from the interior outward, or of currents from the outside toward the interior. Their form is affected, too, by great storms of some kind which sweep over the sun.

Sun spots are not always present, as there may be several days, or possibly weeks, in which none will be seen; they are, however, to be seen during the greater part of the time. Last summer, I may add, was noted for the number of sun spots seen, the newspapers giving frequent accounts of them. It has been discovered that there are certain periods at which they are more numerous than at other times. About every $11\frac{1}{10}$ years in succession they are very numerous; they then become fewer in number for 5 or 6 years, when they begin to increase in number, again, continuing to do so for about the same length of time, or up to the full period of $11\frac{1}{10}$ years. There is, too, a long period, or *cycle* we call it, of about 56 years in which the sun spots

THE ROSE-COLORED ARCH AT SUNSET.

The rosy sunset of November 22, 1885, photographed by Henry C. Maine, showing the rosy arch and the brilliant light below it near the sun.

show this increase, every 56th year of this series being remarkable for the number of the sun spots present.

There seems to be a very close connection between these periods of numerous sun spots and the occurrence of very marked electrical displays here on our earth. Telegraphic and other electrical instruments are sometimes very seriously affected and even for a time rendered useless; it has thus been found impossible, at times, to send messages over the wires. The precise nature of this relation between sun spots and the earth's electrical forces is not understood; when, if ever, it shall be learned, it will no doubt be another source of wonder to us. That strange and beautiful appearance known as the *aurora borealis*, or '*northern lights*,' as it is commonly called, which is seen at night in the northern sky is also affected by the sun spots, being always brightest and presenting the most startling effects at these times of the greatest abundance of the spots. That these northern lights are largely if not wholly of electrical origin is now generally believed.

Some of the older ones among you may remember the wonderful red sunsets or red lights which occurred in the autumn and winter of 1883; I am sure your parents and older brothers and sisters remember them, as they were the common topic of conversation for weeks, and the newspapers were full of the matter, every day. Nothing like these red sunsets has since occurred, nor is it known that they ever occurred before. The light was very bright and reached far up into the sky, continuing, too, long after sunset. Many people were seriously alarmed about the matter, not knowing what caused the fiery skies at night or what it might portend—as, indeed, nobody did. During the day, too, there was a bright circle, or halo, about the sun, while to persons living near the equator the sun appeared of a green color. One explanation since offered is, that our whole atmosphere was filled with a very fine dust or powder, sent up during the eruption of a great volcano—Krakatoa, on the island of Java, in the straits of Sunda—which so affected the sunlight passing through it as to give us the almost blood red glow in the sky after sunset and before sunrise. But it was noticed by astronomers that during the period of a year or more that these red lights were noticed the sun was unusually active, spots were very numerous and great storms swept over its surface.

Mr. Henry Maine, of Rochester, New York, who carefully watched and noted everything connected with these strange appearances, has prepared a paper upon the subject which establishes the fact of a very close and remarkable connection between the appearance of large numbers of sun spots, usually arranged in several groups, and of the great storms on the sun, and the appearance of the red lights and of the occurrence of heavy storms in various parts of the earth. The light was not seen every night, but would occasionally be absent for one or more nights. These periods of absence agreed remarkably with the periods of comparative quiet on the sun; but with the occurrence of another great sun storm or the appearance of a great sun spot or group of spots the red light at once reappeared, storms also occurred, and electrical disturbances of all kinds were very noticeable,— on one occasion even driving telegraph operators from their instruments, in some places, according to the reports, on the day following storms upon the sun. Taking it altogether, his observations go very far to prove the existence of a very close connection, indeed, between sun storms and sun spots and various disturbances upon our planet. Some day, perhaps, the matter will be fully understood; as yet, it but affords material for conjectures, which may finally lead to the discovery of the truth. Scientific men, astronomers, electricians and others, are familiar with this fact of the relation between the sun's spots and storms and our earth-storms, and much has been written in regard to it.

But besides spots there are other curious appearances connected with the sun, many of which are noticed only under special conditions. At the time of an eclipse of the sun, especially, some remarkable appearances are presented.—An eclipse? Well, I'll tell you about eclipses more particularly to-morrow evening, but will only say now that an eclipse of the sun is a hiding from us of a part or the whole of its surface by the moon coming directly between us and the sun—something which occasionally happens. Sometimes the moon does not come so fairly between us and the sun as to hide the whole of the sun, in which case the eclipse is called a partial one; at other times it comes so fairly between us and the sun that the sun is entirely hidden, in which case the eclipse is called a total one. It is at the time of a total eclipse of the sun, that the strange appearances are observed; they are there all the time, I should add, but it is only at the time of an eclipse, when the bright body of the sun which we ordinarily see is covered over and thus hidden by the moon, that we are able to see other parts of it. The sun, as we commonly see it, appears, as you know, as a dazzlingly bright, round body, with no indication of the existence of any other part outside of the perfectly round bright part, or the photosphere, which we see; but when, in an eclipse, the moon hides this round bright part of the sun, there can then be seen surrounding it another part, called the *chromosphere*. This chromosphere is of a red color, being a mass of blazing hydrogen gas extending out from the photosphere, the part of the sun we commonly see, for a distance of 5,000 or 6,000 miles, on all sides—a great ocean of the fiercest fire. Over it sweep storms of such violence that our wildest and most furious hurricanes are tame in comparison. Speaking of these storms Prof. Newcomb, the eminent astronomer, says: 'We must remember that our hurricanes blow only a hundred miles an hour, while those of the chromosphere blow as far in a single second!' and then adds that, should such a hurricane occur on our earth, it would sweep entirely across the United States from the St. Lawrence river to the Gulf of Mexico in half a minute! carrying with it everything upon the earth's surface, cities and towns included, in a mass, 'not simply of ruin, but of glowing vapor, in which the vapors arising from the dissolution of the materials composing the cities of Boston, New York and Chicago would be mixed in a single indistinguishable cloud!' Think of such a fiery storm as should thus in the twinkling of an eye completely, utterly destroy everything, even great cities, leaving only a cloud of vapor of all that was there a moment before! Speaking of the terrific eruptions taking place upon the sun, the same astronomer says: 'When we speak of eruptions, we call to mind Vesuvius burying the surrounding cities in lava, but the solar eruptions, thrown 50,000 miles high, would engulf the earth and dissolve every organized being on its surface in a moment!' These statements give us at least a faint conception of the tremendous activity of the great life-giver of our system—the sun.

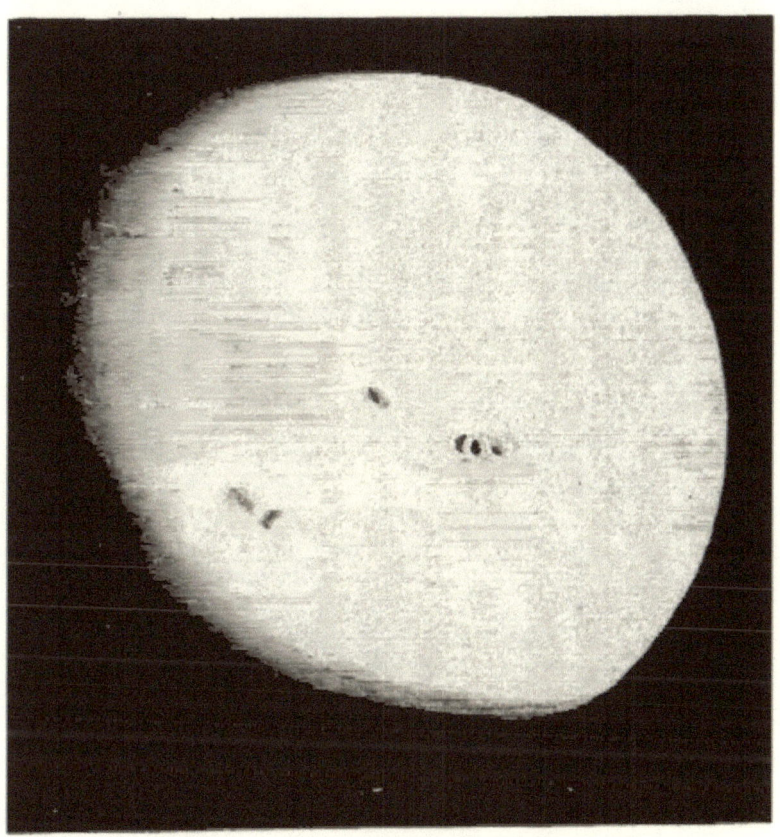

ACTINIC ENERGY ABOUT A SOLAR STORM.

The sun, June 20, 1885, at noon, photographed by Henry C. Maine. The great group of spots was about 110,000 miles long. The actinic energy in the region about the sun storm was so intense that other parts of the sun are left in shadow. Upon the 20th destructive storms swept the northern states.

Whether as a result of the terrific storms or eruptions, or of some other cause, this mass of burning gas, surrounding the sun to the height I have stated—5,000 or 6,000 miles—is often forced outward in parts so as to form as it were great mountains and peaks of flame, rising many thousands of miles above the general surface. These mountains or peaks of red burning gas are called by the astronomers, for want of a more fitting or particular name, prominences or protuberances. They rise, or are forced up rapidly to a height of 50,000 miles—100,000 miles—200,000 miles, or even more, above the general surface of the burning mass, one being observed, in 1880, to reach in a few minutes the tremendous height of 350,000 miles, rising at the astonishing rate of 200 miles a second ! These protuberances of burning gas have various and fantastic shapes. Sometimes they shoot up like jets or plumes, sometimes like great fountains, or, spreading out at the top, take the form of gigantic trees; sometimes they become detached or entirely cut off from the mass of fire below, appearing then as great fiery clouds. They change shape constantly and rapidly, and frequently suddenly appear, shoot upward to a great height, perhaps 50,000 miles or more, and as suddenly disappear, all within a few minutes. Very few of them last more than an hour, although some have been known to last for a number of days. The one which reached the enormous height mentioned a moment ago, after assuming a number of shapes entirely disappeared within two hours of the time it was formed. On one occasion an astronomer, while observing a great prominence which he estimated to be 100,000 miles long and 54,000 miles high, saw it suddenly blown to pieces by some tremendous explosion, the long tongues or sheets of flame into which it was divided by the force of the explosion shooting up to a height of 200,000 miles !

Another feature, and one, too, seen only during the time of a total eclipse, is one of the most remarkable, as it is the most dazzlingly and startlingly beautiful one, connected with our sun. It is what is known as the *corona*, a peculiar and indescribable circle of light which surrounds the sun and extends outward, as sometimes seen, nearly 10,000,000 miles from it. While this strange surrounding brightness may be seen by the naked eye, it is only when viewed through a powerful telescope that its marvelous beauty is revealed. As thus observed, great lines or streams of light are seen shooting far out from the body of the sun (which is then hidden behind the moon), and sometimes assuming a pointed shape, like a huge star. As it is only during the very short time—two or three minutes—when the sun is thus *entirely* hidden by the moon that this wonderful and beautiful appearance, the corona, is to be seen, there is but little time given the astronomer to study it with a view to discovering its nature or cause. Says Prof. Swift: 'No tongue, however eloquent, nor pen, however graphic, can adequately describe those radiant pennons, white as burnished silver, streaming off several hundred thousand miles into space. In the whole range of telescopic vision there is no greater marvel than they present.' Here is a photograph of the corona, taken during the eclipse of 1858, from which we can form a faint idea of the beauty and grandeur of the corona as actually witnessed by the astronomers.

Of course, these strange waving and changing streamers and banners of light, which we call the corona, are always thus about the sun, but it is only during the brief time of the complete hiding of the sun during the eclipse that they can be seen. What the corona is, is largely a mystery, though it is, with good reason, believed to be the reflection of the light from the central body of the sun, by small particles of matter—very minute bodies, or dust or vapor—surrounding the sun to a very great distance. To view the corona and to make other observations, astronomers go thousands of miles, and often to the most out-of-the-way places among mountains or the islands of the ocean, to be at a point, during an eclipse, where the sun will be *entirely* covered by the moon—as only to a very small portion of our earth is the sun

CORONA OF ECLIPSE OF 1858 (BRAZIL).

thus entirely hidden during any eclipse. By the way, such a total eclipse occurred last Sunday, the 22d—No, of course you didn't see it, nor did anybody in the United States. But people within a certain strip of the earth's surface lying in the southern hemisphere, extending from the eastern coast of South America across the Atlantic ocean to Africa saw it, excepting at points where clouds may have interfered. We did not see it here, that is, we had no eclipse here, because the position of the moon was such that it did not come between us and the sun on this part of the earth, although coming between the sun and the part of the earth mentioned; sometimes, however, we see an eclipse while other parts of the world do not, the matter depending entirely upon the position of the earth and moon at the time. We shall probably soon have reports of what was seen, from the astronomers who went from different countries to points from which the eclipse was visible. Great preparations, I may add, were made by our government, and the governments of other countries, to properly view last Sunday's eclipse. The party of astronomers sent out by our government went to a point in the interior of the southern part of Africa, taking with them instruments with which to make various kinds of observations, including photographic apparatus with which to secure pictures of the corona, etc. I will tell you something more about eclipses at another time.

I have already spoken of the zodiacal light, that mysterious luminous appearance which is now believed to surround the sun as a great ring at a distance from it of about 200,000,000 miles, and which is regarded, in a sense, as a part of the sun, or, at least, of its especial surroundings; I need not, therefore, say more about it here."

VIII.

THE SUN:—WHAT IT HAS DONE AND IS DOING FOR US.

"We have, then, briefly considered everything that is known about the sun,—though to tell the truth the greater part of what I have just told you about it is, after all, not known, but only *believed* (though probably correctly) to be as represented. Some day, perhaps, our knowledge may be more full and perfect, as many of earth's most learned men are at work unceasingly, untiringly, seeking to learn the truth in regard to the wonders of the universe so far as it may be possible for man to understand the great Creator's work. You can realize how difficult it is to determine and settle beyond question many points in regard to the sun, when I state that the most powerful telescopes show the sun only as it would appear to our naked eye at a distance of 200,000 miles. Slowly but surely, however, progress has been, and is being made, and one point after another has been, or is being, settled, so that we hope to yet have some of the now doubtful matters made plain to us.

But while we may be in doubt as to what the sun is, how its awful heat has been for ages produced and is still being produced, etc., we are not left in doubt as to many of the wonderful effects of the heat and light which it is constantly sending out to us and to all the planets and other bodies included in our system of worlds. I have already stated that, without the sun's heat and light, our world would be cold and dead, utterly devoid of life, but we are not only indebted

to the sun for sustaining our lives day by day, but we are directly
indebted to it, and to an extent which we cannot even begin to esti-
mate, for this same life-giving and life-sustaining energy sent out, as
it is still being sent out, to-day, through perhaps many millions of
years. We are receiving every day in many ways, though all unknown
to perhaps the majority of people, the benefit of the heat and light
which our earth received from the sun ages ago, when the earth was
being prepared and fitted up as a dwelling place for man. It is,
strange as it may seem, the sunshine of ages ago which is this
moment giving us warmth and light in this pleasant room—it is the
sunshine of ages ago which thus gives warmth and light to homes
all over our earth, which drives all our machinery, and which carries
us in railroad trains and steamships to any part of the world, or
around it, for that matter. The long-ago sunshine has simply been
bottled up, as it were, in—Oh, yes; I see you have n't forgotten, Ned,
what we learned two or three years ago in regard to the origin of
petroleum and natural gas, coal and similar substances. As some of
you were not with us in our excursion to the oil and gas fields, three
years ago, and to the coal fields the following year, I suppose I should
explain, briefly, some things which the others of you had explained
to you, more fully, at the time. The great beds of coal which we now
find more or less deeply buried in the earth, beneath beds of rock,
were at one time, long before man was created—ages ago, indeed—
great and dense forests or jungles of tropical trees and plants—ferns,
etc.—growing upon what was then the surface of the earth, and
deriving their life and growth from the sunshine which streamed off
from the sun then as it does now. Later, these forests sank by reason
of great earthquakes or other disturbances, and the waters of the
ocean swept in over them, carrying with them sand, etc., which
covered the sunken forests. In the course of a long—a very, very
long—time, these beds of sand, etc., thus washed in, became the
great beds or layers of rock which we now find on top of the coal-beds,
while at the same time, the buried forests or jungles were as slowly
changed by reason of the great pressure of these rock beds above and
by heat received in part from this pressure and in part from the fiery
interior of the earth, into what are now our beds of coal.

These changes, of which it has taken me but a minute to tell you,
occupied a wonderfully long period—such a number of years, according to the geologists, as you could not comprehend should I give it.
However, I think you will understand the point I wish to make—that
the sunshine of ages ago formed the beautiful trees and ferns of the
forests and jungles; that these, deeply buried in the earth, were
changed into coal; and that to-day the brave and brawny men who
spend so great a part of their lives in the dark and dismal mines, so
far from the beautiful sunshine, are really digging out, in the great,
rough blocks of coal, sunshine itself—the sunshine of millions of years

ago, bottled or locked up in the black coal-beds that we may enjoy the blessings of its use, to-day! How wonderfully GOD has provided for us! When, therefore, we burn our coal in our stoves or grates to warm our houses, or in the form of gas to light them, or burn it in the furnaces of mills and factories, or under the boilers of the locomotives or steamships which carry us wherever we may choose to go, we are after all, simply using sunshine—we are simply getting back from the coal, as GOD designed we should, the heat and light which His sun-shine put into the trees and ferns of so long, long ago. It is a wonderful truth—and truth as beautiful as wonderful. It sounds like a fairy-story—but who ever heard fairy-story half so wonderful?

So, too, with the oil and gas pouring from the wells we visited —produced, as we have the best reasons to believe, from those same old-time forests, and by the same causes, which produced the coal, the heavier part we now call coal remaining where it was first buried and the lighter part escaping as oil or gas to the beds of porous rock from which we get them through the wells drilled to them. Our lamplight is, then, really sunlight—the sun still brightly shining in the dark hours of the night, long after he has disappeared behind the western hills, but shining with the bright beams sent to our earth and into the trees and plants untold ages ago! From the oil fields of Pennsylvania is sent, in rough cans or barrels, to the uttermost parts of the earth, what we call petroleum, or oil; but it is really GOD's beautiful sunshine, stored up for us all these years—and only GOD himself can measure the sunshine of cheerfulness and comfort which this real sunshine from Pennsylvania's oil-wells has brought into millions of homes the world over!

It would seem, and we can readily believe, that as nothing has been created in vain, so nothing is lost, in GOD's great universe. The same sunshine which streams down to us to-day streamed down to our earth, we are told, millions of years ago; yet it was not lost, but is enjoyed by us, to-day, in many ways—indeed, we could not do without it. We can believe, then, that the vast amount of energy, in the form of heat and light, which goes streaming out into space un-ceasingly—our earth and all the bodies of our system combined receiving, as I have already told you, but a small portion of it as compared with the mighty tide which flows between them—we can believe, I say, that this all has its use and purpose, though it be un-known to us.

How far into space the sun's heat and light travel—how far its influence extends and is felt, are questions far beyond our power to answer. To what unimaginable distances must the swift-flying comets go, that it should be ten years—a hundred years—a thousand years—yes more than a hundred thousand years, as calculated for some of them, before they again get back to the sun! and yet the sun's power has followed these roving children of his in their wonderful flight, and finally brings them back again to be held, as it were, close to his great warm heart for a little time, as they swing around him, before they speed away again upon their journey—to us unknown, but marked by Him who 'sitteth on the circle of the heavens'!

How this all-controlling power of the sun which enables him to hold the planets, the comets, etc., in their courses, though flying through space with tremendous speed and at distances of multiplied millions of miles from him, permitting them to go just so far away from him and then drawing them back again, so as to cause them to forever circle round and round him nor ever 'swing an inch out of place, nor a second out of time,' is a deep question, indeed. True, we say it is by the law of gravitation. But what, then, is gravitation?—simply a name which we have given to something which we do not understand. We know that there is a law of the universe which causes all bodies to attract all other bodies—and the discovery of the existence of this law has made Newton's name immortal; we see, too, and can calculate, the effects produced by this law, and although we do not understand how it is exerted, we must have a name for it by which we may speak of it, and so we call it gravitation,—just as we call another force, the existence of which we know, and the workings of which we see, but do not understand, electricity. But, after all, these are but names, convenient terms by which we may speak of these great forces—and by the use of which we may not only express the little we know about these things, but sometimes conceal our ignorance concerning the much we have yet to learn.

But a name, only, does not satisfy us—we want to know all that is back of it. To tell an intelligent man who has never heard of the steam engine—supposing we could find such a man, these days—that the hundreds of machines of various kinds, in a great factory, were driven by steam, would not satisfy him—not at all. Not seeing any steam about the machines, and knowing, further, that steam, of itself, could not make these machines run, he would at once seek to learn how the steam was made to do this work, and how and by whom its power was directed. So, when we behold with amazement the perfect working of the far more wonderful machinery, as we may term it, of the great universe, and are told that all its parts are controlled by gravitation, we are not satisfied with the answer—we want to know how and by whom this force called gravitation is directed. We behold, first, our own system, with its great central sun, around which constantly circle eight great worlds, with their moons, hundreds of smaller worlds, the asteroids—'pocket-worlds,' some one calls them—millions of the far-ranging comets, and millions of millions of those tiny bodies which are too small to be seen only as they flash out as meteors or shooting stars as they pass through our atmosphere—we see all this, and we wonder; we are, next, to think of our wonderful system as but one of unnumbered millions of such systems, being told by the astronomers that each of the far-away stars is a sun, like ours, and probably surrounded by a similar system of circling worlds, etc.—and our wonder grows; further, we are told that just as the worlds circle around the sun, in each system, so each one of these numberless systems, our own included, is, as a whole, itself in motion, all circling, in vast orbits, around some far, far-distant center—and growing wonder turns to amazement; and, finally, when we consider that it is the attraction back and forth between all these bodies, great and small, of all these countless systems that holds our own world and each and every body of all this mighty and ever swiftly-flying host so delicately yet so securely poised in space that not one can ever go astray, our amazement is unbounded: knowing, now, that the elements which compose the worlds as we see these elements in the form of rocks or earth, or water or gases—things which we may use as we please every day —knowing that these have no power of themselves to thus uphold themselves and to guide and control all the multiplied and complex movements of the universe, we, like the man who is simply told that steam moves the wonderful machinery he sees, are not satisfied with the answer made to our wondering inquiry—we are not satisfied to be told simply that all this wonderful work we behold is the result of what is called the law of gravitation, we want to know who directs and controls the workings of this wonderful law—the great Master Mechanic who constructed this wonderful machinery of the universe and controls its marvelous workings—and we are brought face to face with the truth that it all can be the perfect handiwork of only the one all-wise and all-powerful GOD the CREATOR!"

IX.

THE WONDERS OF THE SUNBEAM.

"One of the most curious as well as wonderful things connected with the sun, is the manner in which its light and heat are carried to our earth and elsewhere throughout our system, and as far beyond as it may reach. They are brought to us from the sun by vibrations, as they are called, or, in other words, in the form of tiny waves—waves too tiny, indeed, for us to form an idea of their tininess, their wonderful littleness, there being more than 64,000 of these little waves or vibrations within the length of a single inch, in the case of the waves or vibrations which give us the color of violet—each color throughout the whole range of the numberless shades and tints, as in flowers and ribbons, being produced, I should state, by a difference in the number of these tiny waves or vibrations of light, each shade having its own number. Ah, yes! I thought that would interest you—especially the girls. I suppose I shall have to try to answer some of your questions about the matter, but won't promise to answer all, as I don't want to talk all night.

I may begin by stating that heat and motion are, in a very important sense, the same thing. Heat means motion—it is a form of motion. Any heated body, as, for instance, a bar of red-hot iron, is in motion within itself, though we may not see this motion—its particles swinging and striking against each other with the greatest rapidity, the whole body being in a tremble, as it were, or, more properly speaking, in a state of rapid or intense vibration. Our sun, being so highly heated, is thus in a state of the most intense vibration, and the light and heat come to us thus in tiny waves or vibrations, as I told you, because of the vibration of the sun itself. I should tell you that space—which I have called emptiness, and which may in a sense be even so considered— is filled with a something which is called ether (but not the liquid ether you get at the drug store) and it is the vibrations of this ether given to it by the vibrating sun which bring to us the sun's light and heat. The light and heat come to us thus together, but only the more rapid vibrations give us light. In the sunshine which falls upon and around us there are to be found seven colors, though as the sunshine comes to us these colors are all combined so that it is simply white light. But by passing this white sunlight through a three-sided piece of glass, called a prism —most of you, I suppose, have seen prisms and have looked through them to see the rainbow colors—by passing sunshine through such a piece of glass the colors of which the light is composed are separated, and we have seven colors instead of the simple white light of the sunshine, as before. These colors run from red through orange, yellow, green, blue and indigo to violet, red being the color produced by a rapidity of vibrations less than that of any of the others, and violet by the most rapid vibrations of which our eyes can catch the color. A piece of iron placed in the fire first becomes red, after it has become so hot as to vibrate with the degree of rapidity which produces the red color, while, if we increase its heat the number of vibrations will be increased in proportion until we might run through the whole scale of colors. Color, I should tell you, is altogether in our eyes, not in the things we see, and which we say are red or blue, as the case may be; color is produced in the eye as the effect of the falling upon it of the vibrations of light, the different rates of rapidity of the vibrations giving the effect of different colors, a certain number of vibrations always producing the same color in the eye. The rapidity of the vibrations of light as it is carried to us from the sun is astonishing, indeed. The effect of red is produced in our eyes by the falling upon them of as many as 392,000,000,000,000 vibrations every second! while, still more marvelous, 754,000,000,000,000 vibrations every second produce the effect of violet!—the other shades named, as well as all other imaginable tints being produced by numbers of vibrations between those producing red and violet. Every moment, excepting when we have our eyes closed or are in the dark, this wonderful tide of vibrations is surging against our eyes, the combinations changing with every movement of our eyes, which brings new objects into view. Think of the number of vibrations that must pour into our eyes every instant while looking at a bouquet or bed of many colored flowers, at our pictures or carpets, or—most gorgeous of all—this piece of 'crazy' patch-work, which is the delight of womankind old and young.

And yet, as I have already said, color is altogether in our eyes. This ribbon at Nell's throat has no color of its own; but it receives and holds all the vibrations which come to it from the sun—or from this gas light which, after all, is old-time sunshine, as I have told you—it receives all vibrations excepting the 653,000,000,000,000 per second which produce a certain color, and these it reflects or throws back, producing that color in our eyes, and we say the ribbon is blue. This spot in the carpet we say is green, because it receives and holds all vibrations but the 610,000,000,000,000 per second which are reflected, and entering our eye produce the effect of green,—and so it is with any other color. Light travels at the wonderful speed of about 186,000 miles per second; so, every second there enters our eyes, in the form of these tiny waves or vibrations, a stream of light 186,000 miles long! Traveling at this rate, it requires but a little more than eight minutes for a wave of light leaving the sun to reach our earth, so that while we should watch the sun for that brief time, a stream of light equal to our distance of nearly 93,000,000* miles from the sun would come dashing, wave after wave, into our eyes!

Our heat comes to us with our light, though the vibrations which produce the effect of the colors in our eye—the *colorific* or color vibrations, we call them—bring to us less heat than do other vibrations which we cannot see as we can see the color vibrations. The vibrations producing the violet color bring the least heat, the amount increasing down through the list to those producing red, which is the warmest color. But the greater part of our heat is brought to us, as I have said, by vibrations which come to us less rapidly than those which are able to produce the effect of color, and are, therefore, not seen; and just as there are different shades of color, as produced by different degrees of rapidity in the color vibrations, so there are different kinds of heat, produced by a difference of rapidity in what we call the *calorific* or heat vibrations. The longer and slower the vibrations the greater the amount of heat they bring. This accounts for the fact that the violet vibrations, being the shortest and most

* The distance of the sun, as determined by the most recent calculations, is between 92,500,000 and 93,000,000 miles, which accounts for the fact that some writers use the first-named, others the last-named, number when giving the sun's distance.

rapid of the color vibrations, show the least heat, the amount increasing as the vibrations become a little larger and less rapid through the various colors down to red, the vibrations of which color are the largest and least rapid of any we can see. The unseen vibrations are still larger and slower than the red color vibrations, down through the different kinds of heat to that which is the most fierce.

As light passes through glass without in any way affecting the glass, so heat passes through some bodies without affecting them. And as a flower or bit of ribbon reflects the vibrations which give to it its color in our eye, receiving and absorbing all the other vibrations, so some bodies allow some kinds of heat vibrations to pass through them without either being affected, but will absorb all the vibrations of other kinds of heat, holding them and thereby becoming heated. Then, too, the heat vibrations which come to us with the color vibrations, as in sunshine, can go where the other or dark heat vibrations cannot go—a matter of the utmost importance to us, and showing, again, the wisdom of Him who created us and all things. Sunshine passes unchecked through our air, carrying the heat of the sun to us, and giving it up to the earth as the vibrations strike against it, warming it and thus giving and sustaining life. The earth thus heated, throws off its heat again, but as dark heat. Now, if this dark heat could pass through our air as can the luminous heat of the sunshine in coming to us, it would escape at night as rapidly as it was received during the day, and our nights, even at the equator, would be colder than the polar regions—the earth would be unfit for our habitation. As it is, however, the heat which came through the air, in the sunshine, cannot, except to a limited extent, pass out again through it, so that the earth carries over with it into and through the night a large measure of the heat which it receives during the day, and life is thus sustained. Who but an all-wise Being could have so arranged this and the thousands of other wonderful things essential to our life and happiness, which appear to us as we inquire into nature's laws and forces? It is the operation of this same law, too, that makes our houses so much more comfortable than the streets on such a cold day as this. If the heat from our fire could fly out through our windows as easily as the heat from the sun comes in, in the sunshine, this would be a most uncomfortable party, I assure you,—a chilliness would indeed be thrown over us, as Joe feared there might be the other day, you know. We should, were there no such provision as I have named, be compelled to board up or otherwise cover our windows during cold weather; for, if left as they now are, ' we might as well,' as Bishop Warren puts it in his most entertaining book on astronomy*,—' we might as well try to heat our rooms with the window-panes all out, and the blast of winter sweeping through them.'

---

*Recreations in Astronomy.

I must add, however, that besides the vibrations giving us light and heat there are in our sunshine other vibrations, called *actinic* or chemical vibrations, which are also great wonder-workers and without whose wonder-working presence and power our world, warmed and lighted as it might be by the other classes of vibrations, those of heat and color, would be very incomplete—indeed, a barren desert. Without these vibrations, the farmer, the gardener, the fruit grower, the florist all would toil in vain. The farmer prepares his ground, applying fertilizers and plowing it; this done, he sows or plants his seed, and then—waits; he can do nothing more to insure a harvest—he can only wait. But what he cannot do, strong man that he is, these vibrations, though so very, very little that scores of thousands of them are gathered within the length of a single inch, can do for him with perfect ease. The rains water his fields, and the sunshine falls upon them, and the warmth and moisture soon cause the seeds to swell and sprout, and from the death and decay of the old seed sown by the farmer, there springs into life a new plant—a marvelous thing, a change which man not only cannot bring about, but which he cannot even understand. And now what is going on? The chemical rays or vibrations of the sun are busily at work; they are taking hold of the elements, nitrogen, potash, etc., which go to make the growing plant, as it finds them in the soil itself, or in the fertilizers which the farmer has applied, selecting them and separating them from other elements with unerring accuracy, and in some mysterious way feeding it to the young plant, continuing their unseen, unheard but wonderful work days, weeks, months, aided by the rains and by the warmth of the heat vibrations, until we have ' first the blade, then the ear, and afterward the full corn in the ear'; and then the glad reapers go forth and gather in the rich harvest which these busy, skillful fingers of the sunshine have produced from the seed sown in doubt and uncertainty, perhaps,—from 'some an hundred-fold, some sixty-fold, some thirty-fold.' 'What hath GOD wrought?' we may well exclaim, as we contemplate not only what we may call the greater wonders of His universe, but the wonders which lie, often un-suspected, everywhere about us and which defy not only our utmost skill to reproduce, but even our greatest wisdom to comprehend them,—every-day miracles, we may well term them.

As with our grain, so, too, with our vegetables, our fruits and our flowers. These tiny, miracle-working fingers of the sunshine select from the soil the elements needed for the growth of each—this for a potato, that for a radish, another for a cabbage!—this for a peach, that for an apple, another for a grape or berry!—this for a violet, that for a daisy, another for the beautiful golden-rod!—this for a white rose, that for a red one, another for a yellow one!—and so on, with unerring skill, through all the realm of plants and fruits and flowers! Think for a moment of the marvelous skill displayed in the coloring of even a single beautifully-marked pansy—to say nothing of the almost endless variety of these little beauties growing side by side and in the same soil, in a single bed. It is the chemical vibrations, too, which enable the photographer to accomplish his wonderful work, whereby, in the fraction of a second, one's face or some beautiful view is indelibly traced on the glass plate in the camera, and from which hundreds of pictures can then be printed.

Yes, indeed, Ned,—very wonderful. And I might tell you very many more most curious and wonderful things in regard to light and heat, of what they do for us and how they do it, so far as we under-stand it, etc., etc., but we have not time to speak of all the particulars concerning these things, of which you will, I trust, seek to learn all that may be learned, as you become older. You will remember, too, that I would n't promise to answer all your questions,—and so will stop, right here.

And I must close my talk about the sun, in general, too, though very much more might be said upon a great many, indeed upon all, the points I have more or less briefly mentioned; however, it is not my purpose to give you, for the most part, more than the prrincipal facts in regard to these matters, but I shall hope that what you have heard will lead you to read and study as much as you may be able in regard to not only the wonders of astronomy, but those of chemistry, natural philosophy, geology, etc. You will find such reading and study very much more valuable than the reading to which too many boys and girls give their time, and you will find many of the books upon the subjects I have mentioned highly entertaining,—at least I find them so.

Well, the meeting is adjourned, as the big people say at the close of their meetings. To-morrow night we will have a little moonshine; come early, as our moon will rise promptly at seven o'clock, and will set—well, whenever we are done with it.

Good night, Miss Inquisitive—good night, all."

X.

THE MOON:—ITS APPEARANCE AND PHASES.

"Good evening, youngsters; all here, I believe, even ahead of time. Well, so much the better, as we can be in readiness to begin our talk at the time set, instead of only beginning our preparations at that time. Now, the rest of you get your places, while Ned and myself arrange the blinds and curtains of these windows so that we all can look out, skyward, as we may wish to do, after awhile. That's good;—now we are ready to begin, and just in time, too, as our clock is about to strike seven,—there it goes, now.

I said our moon would rise at seven o'clock, by which I meant, as some of you may have guessed, that our moon talk would begin at that hour. The moon itself, however, rose at a much earlier hour, so that now, as we see, it is already high up in the sky; it rose at a few minutes after one, this afternoon, but, on account of the greater brightness of the sunshine, we could not see it at that time nor for several hours afterward, when, as the sun and his intense brightness disappeared in the west, the moon was seen—already far above the horizon—very faint at first, but growing brighter as the twilight deepened, until now it is shining with a splendor of silvery brightness which, softly touching hilltop and valley, wood and stream, causes us to rapturously cry, 'Oh, what a beautiful night!' I may add that yesterday the moon rose about twelve o'clock, or a little more than an hour earlier than it rose to-day, while to-morrow it will rise more than an hour later than it did to-day, or considerably after two o'clock —I'll explain the matter a little later, young lady.

The moon-is, as it always has been, a most interesting object,— as, too, it has been, is, and probably will long continue to be, the subject of numberless more or less interesting essays, lectures, talks, poems, stories, jokes, queer superstitions, still queerer opinions and all kinds of the queerest of notions. Of course, you all are acquainted, in a way, with that strange personage the 'Man in the Moon'—all boys and girls are. Some of you, perhaps, have heard or seen in newspapers some allusion to the old joke about the moon being made of green cheese; and, possibly, have, too, heard or seen something spoken of as 'moonshine'—which is a very common way of expressing our opinion that some other person's opinion or statement about some matter is not worth very much. There is, I may add, a very great deal of this kind of 'moonshine' in regard to the moon itself—the superstitions and queer notions to which I alluded, a moment ago. None, perhaps, is more time-honored and familiar than the nonsense in regard to the good or bad luck which we may expect, according to which shoulder it may be over which we happen to first see a new moon. The younger people, now-a-days are disposed to count as 'moonshine,' and to make fun of, the beliefs or notions to which their fathers and grandfathers hold with unwavering faith. Many old farmers, especially, are learned in these matters—in moon-lore, as we term it—and are guided by it, almost entirely, in their farming operations. They firmly believe that some things, to be done right, must be done in the 'light of the moon,' others in the 'dark of the moon,' this or that thing when the moon is new, or full, or in first or last quarter, as the case may be, and that their labor will be lost, or its results be more or less disastrously unsatisfactory, if any kind of work is performed 'in the wrong time of the moon.' There is to them a right and wrong time to sow or plant, and to cut their grass and grain, to cut down trees for certain uses, to pick their apples, to set their posts in the ground, to kill their pigs—in fact, to do almost any-thing and everything, and they are ready to prove, by past experience, that their beliefs are well grounded. The changes of the weather, too, depend, they believe, very largely, if not entirely, upon the moon's changes or phases, or upon its special position when first seen, as the new moon, each month; but observations made for the purpose of testing the matter are said to disprove this belief, so that it is the opinion of astronomers that the moon has but little, if any, influence on the matter. As to its influence, so widely believed in, touching the other matters I have mentioned, and many more, astronomers do not share the beliefs so commonly held.

That the moon has power to affect and influence the earth in cer-tain ways, as in causing the tides, is well known, but whether success or failure in such everyday matters as those I have mentioned depends upon the moon, is something we may well doubt. In connection with this subject, I may mention that it is the general belief that crazy per-sons are greatly affected by the moon, being much worse during the time when the moon appears largest and brightest—full moon, we term it. Indeed, it is this general belief which has given us the common term used in speaking of such unfortunate people—lunatics, a word which comes from the Latin name of the moon, *luna*. But here, again, observations made to test the matter do not, we are told, agree with the common opinion. I have read, too, some strange and start-ling accounts of the terrible results experienced by sailors who have slept on the decks of their vessels, and soldiers or hunters who have slept upon the plains, uncovered, in the full glare of the full moon. How much or how little of all these beliefs in regard to the moon's influence upon our affairs, great and small, is true, I do not pretend to say; I simply give them to you, as matters about which you may often hear, as you grow older. What is true, we ought to know, with certainty; what is only 'moonshine' should be chased away with the sunshine of the truth, fully established. I must not forget to add, in leaving this matter, that it is a standing joke that lovers are particularly interested in the moon, and particularly affected by it. Whether this is true or not nobody knows but the lovers—and they, of course, won't tell.—Do I ? Now, Miss Inquisitive, how do you suppose an old bachelor like me could know ?

But what is the moon about which there are so many curious notions ? Well, it is a world, in shape round like the earth, but much smaller in size, suspended in space, as are all the worlds, etc., traveling around the sun in company with our earth, and at the same time, too, circling round and round the earth, just as the earth and the other planets all the time circle round and round the sun. There comes into my mind, while thus telling you what the moon is, the funny opening stanza of a laughable story in rhyme, which appeared in one of our school books, when I was somewhat younger, and which I might have given you instead of the statement I did give you.—Let you have it, anyhow? Oh, it's hardly worth while, now; still, as it is a funny little thing in its way, and will afford us a pleasant and innocent little laugh, which is something we all need, occasionally, perhaps, I'll let you have it, especially as it contains, if not more, certainly as much, truth as poetry. There are but four lines of it, so we shall not lose much time with it, anyhow. The rhymester, to introduce his tale, first tells us :—

‘ The moon it is a great, big world,
    And hangs up in the sky ; ’

and having given us this piece of truthful information he naively adds:—

‘ And giveth light, on moonlight nights,
    To the worlds a-passing by.’

Ah ! I thought that would tickle you—Joe, especially, seems delighted ; I suspect the odd statement that the moon gives light *on moonlight nights* is what particularly pleases him. Now, you've had your poetry, and your laugh,—let us get to work again.

The diameter of the moon is a little over one-fourth that of the earth, being about 2,160 miles. Our earth is about 50 times as large as the moon. The moon's average distance from us is about 238,000 miles —quite a long distance, of course, but a very small one as compared with our distance from the sun and from the other bodies of our system, so that we may consider our moon as quite a near neighbor. As the moon's path or orbit around the earth, like the orbit of the earth and all the other bodies, is not a perfect circle, but an ellipse, the moon is brought closer to us at some times than at others, just as the earth is sometimes closer to, sometimes farther from, the sun, as it swings around it.

While all the bodies of our system belong first to the sun, yet the moon may be said to belong more particularly to our earth, as it is the great power of the earth's attraction—so great on account of its nearness and much greater size—that holds the moon so close to us, and

compels it to circle round us, unceasingly. It thus circles or revolves
about our earth once in about a month—from which comes the division
of the year into months, the word month itself coming from the word
moon. The time of a revolution of the moon does not, however,
exactly correspond to our months, being but about 29½ days, so that
during our year of 365¼ days, the moon makes nearly 12½ revolutions
around the earth; so, if we still counted our time by moons, as some
savages do, without taking the additional days into the account, we
should find, pretty soon, that things did not agree, that they were very
badly mixed up, indeed, as we would be gaining time, as it were, quite
rapidly.

So you thought, Bess, that the moon goes around the earth every
day—as it was believed, a few centuries ago, that the sun thus goes
daily around us. They certainly both appear to thus go around us,
disappearing behind the western hills and coming up again from behind the eastern ones; but we have learned that it is the turning of the
earth itself entirely round each day that makes it appear that the sun
and moon revolve around us. The moon does go around the earth,
it is true, but only once in nearly a month, as we have just learned,
instead of every day.

Ah, yes, Miss Inquisitive, you've asked the question I was expecting, in some form, from you or from some one of the others. What
becomes of the moon during a part of each month is a puzzling matter
to very many older heads than yours, although the explanation of its
apparent disappearance is very simple. The truth is, the moon does
not leave us, at all, as it appears to do, but remains in our company,
following its regular monthly path around us, whether we see it or not.
The reason it thus regularly appears and disappears, growing larger,
as it seems, each night that it is seen, is owing to the fact
that it is not a self-luminous body, like the sun—that is, it does not produce its own light as does the sun—but depends for its light and heat,
as do all the other bodies of our system, upon the sun. If it were like
the sun we would see it during a part of every twenty-four hours, as
we do the sun. But the brightness of the moon—the moonshine which
we receive from it—is really the sunshine which falls upon the moon,
reflected or thrown off again from the moon and coming then to us—
sunshine at second hand as it were, as is, too, the light we receive from
Venus, Jupiter, and all the planets of our system.

As the moon swings around us, in its monthly journey, it will, of
course, be sometimes in the same direction from us as is the sun, and
at other times on exactly the other side of the earth from the sun, and
at yet other times at different positions between these points. As
moonlight is, after all, simply sunlight reflected to us from the surface
of the moon, we can get moonlight only from the part of the moon on
which the sun is shining—that you can clearly see; you can see, too, that
we can get moonlight from only as much of even the side of the moon

on which the sun is shining as happens to be turned toward or facing our earth, which is the reason, as I will explain in a moment, why we see more of the moon at some times than at others, while at other times we do not see it at all. The whole of the side of the moon facing the sun, or one-half of the whole globe of the moon, is all the time illuminated by the sun, just as is one-half of our earth, as it turns round and round on its axis; but, owing to the different positions occupied by the moon as it circles around us, it is only once a month that we are able to see the whole of the bright side of the moon, the side upon which the sun is shining, while at other times we can see only a part of this illuminated side, or, again, are unable to see any of it. I'll illustrate this, calling our lamp the sun, and using Bess' head for a moon—she'll make quite a handsome one, too.—Come, Joe, no more of that; you mustn't make jokes about our new moon.

Stand just here, Bess, between us and the lamp, and facing it— I'll pull it up a little, so as to bring it a little above your head, so. Now, we have it, only we are to remember that the sun is ever and ever so many times larger than the moon. When you move, Bess, as I shall direct, you are to keep your face always toward the lamp. Now, one-half of Bess' head—her face, as she is placed—is illuminated by the light of the lamp, just as half of the real moon is lighted by the real sun. But as the bright half—her face—is turned away from us as it faces the sun (the dark or night half—the back of her head—being turned toward us) we cannot see our moon at all. We can, to be sure, see the back of Bess' head, in our illustration here in our little room, but in the case of the real sun and moon, the very great brightness of the sunshine streaming past it to us, as the lamplight comes to us over her head, so fills all space and our eyes as to prevent us from seeing the dark side of the little round moon passing a little below it, as in our illustration, or a little above it, as is often the case. So, we cannot see the moon at all at such a time, which is called the time of *new moon.* As the moon is constantly moving on along its path—just as I am having Bess to slowly move now, still facing the lamp—it passes out from the position it occupies at new moon, getting farther to one side of the sun all the time, but still covered up as it were by his brightness, and thus hidden from us for two or three days, being then first seen by us in the west, just after sunset, as a narrow little crescent-shaped strip of silvery light,—a discovery which boys and girls usually announce by shouting—'Oh, *I* see the new moon!' Bess, now, is about in the position as regards the lamp that the moon is in as regards the sun, at the time we first see the silvery crescent—we can, you notice, see just a little strip of her face, as illuminated by the lamplight, or sunlight, as we are to suppose. As she moves on around in the circle, we can, you see, catch a little more of her bright face every moment, just as we see more of the bright side of the moon, night after night, as it moves around us in its monthly path—her position just now, by the way, being about exactly that of the real moon, as we see it through the window there. In about a week from new moon it has moved to a point corresponding with Bess' present position, one-fourth of the way around, in which position we can see just one-half of the sunshiny side, just as we can now see one-half of Bess' lamp-lighted face. As this half of the bright side which we see is, of course, one-fourth or one-quarter of the whole moon, the moon is said to have now reached *first quarter.*

The moon still moving on—we shall have to turn round a little to watch *our* moon now—still moving on around its nearly circular path, we are enabled to see more and more of its bright face, every night (as we see more of Bess' bright face every moment), now the side that was first hollow, and afterward, as at first quarter, straight, now bulging out, as it · ere. This shape of the moon is called *gibbous*—a term which means more than a quarter but less than a half circle—as we can see more than a quarter of the moon, but not the full half, or the whole of its bright side. A little later, or in a little more than two weeks from the time of new moon, the moon has reached the point corresponding to the position Bess now occupies—it has passed half way around its orbit and is exactly opposite the starting point of new moon, though, as we see, it is now on the other side of the earth from the sun, which it exactly faces again, as at the new moon point, the sun shining past our earth upon it. Looking from the earth now, as we are looking at Bess, we can see the whole of the bright half of the moon, just as we can see the whole of the bright half of Bess' head—her full, bright face—and we say now that the moon is *full.*

Still moving on—for it never stops—the moon gets off to one side again, as it were, and now we see less and less of its bright side, it growing smaller exactly at the same rate at which it before grew larger —showing, of course, as much of the bright part at any point on this side of its course, as it did at the corresponding point on the other side, as it left the sun, but now turned in the opposite direction. When it has reached the position Bess now occupies, we can see but half the bright side, again, or one-fourth of the whole moon, and the moon is said to have now reached its *third* or *last quarter.* From this point, which is, of course, exactly opposite the first quarter point, the moon moves on in between us and the sun, showing less and less of its bright side, as we see less of Bess' face, until only the narrow crescent is left; then this, too, disappears, as the moon is again hidden by the sun's brightness, and two or three days later the moon is back, as is Bess, at the starting point, and we have new moon, again,—and as one moon is enough for ordinary occasions, Bess is excused from further service, with our thanks, of course, for her very excellent personation of 'Fair Luna,' as the poets call her.

I will make a picture showing these changes of the moon, or its *phases,* as they are called. Here is the earth following its path around

the sun—which we will indicate by this dotted line; this other dotted
line I am making around the earth—so—represents the moon's path—
and, now, we are ready to place the moon at various points so as to
show its phases, beginning wih new moon.

New moon, you know, is when the moon comes between us and the
sun—as it did very early last Sunday morning—passing along either
a little higher or lower than the sun except at the time of an eclipse,
when it comes fairly between us and the sun, as I will soon explain.
We will show the new moon, then, up here, supposing the sun to be

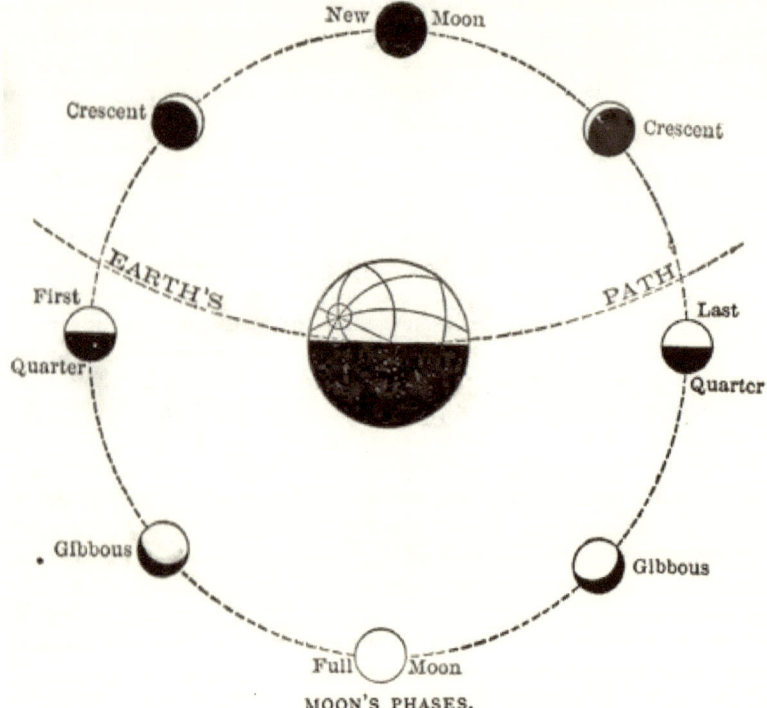

MOON'S PHASES.

shining from above. Looking from the earth we have this dark side
turned toward us, as you notice—though we cannot see it as we can
in my picture, on account of the sun's great brightness, as already
told you. But two or three days later, the moon moving on in this direction—toward the left, as does the earth—we see the young moon
as a little silvery crescent after sunset,—as some of you may have seen
it, two or three evenings ago; this will be at about this point in our
picture, where I will now put it. Of course the sun is still shining, and
always shines, on the whole of one side of the moon—as the lamp did
on Bess' whole face—but we can see only the part, much or little, which

faces toward us as the moon goes around us. More of it shows, of course, each day, as you have often noticed, perhaps, until in a little more than a week, when it is one-fourth of the way around, we see half of the bright side, or one-fourth of the whole moon, as I before explained, and the moon is at first quarter, as we will represent it, just here—the point which, I may state, that real, bright moon, out yonder will reach a little after midnight of to-morrow night. When at the point of first or last quarter the moon is said to be in *quadrature;* when at new moon, I should add, it is said to be in *conjunction* with the sun, and when at full moon to be in *opposition* to the sun.

If you will watch the moon, now, night after night, you will notice it rising later, and later, taking on the gibbous or bulged shape—as I will show, here—until, having reached this point, just half way around from new moon, its full, bright side fairly faces both the sun and our earth, and we see the full moon—here. It will by this time be rising so late at night that boys and girls of your size will hardly have a chance to watch it any longer unless, waking up between midnight and morning, you should go to your window for a sight of it. Should you do so, you would find less and less of the bright side could be seen each night, being turned further away from the earth, as it keeps on its course, until having passed into the gibbous shape again, and through it, it would at this point, the last quarter, show but one-half the bright side, again,—so. However, it would now be rising but a little before sunrise, and you might be unable to see it, while beyond this point, rising still longer after sunrise each day, you could not see it at all. Could you still watch it, however, you would see it take the crescent shape again, as here, in our picture, and rapidly become smaller until, coming in between us and the sun again, it would be lost in his brightness, and, about 29½ days after it left the new moon point, it would be back there again—only to keep right on, again, going through the same changes of appearance, month after month, year after year, as it has been doing—well, we cannot even guess how long.

The moon, as I have said, is about 29½ days in going from new moon to new moon; it makes the circuit of the earth, however, in only about 27⅓ days, but as the earth has been at the same time rapidly moving on in its own orbit, the moon must travel an additional two days and more, in order to catch up and come again fairly into the new-moon position.

It is the movement of the moon around the earth which causes it to rise later each night—or day, when it rises at such time. It was this matter Miss Inquisitive asked, awhile ago, to have explained. Well, if the moon did not move around the earth, but kept the same position, always, it would rise at the same time all the year round. As it is the turning of the earth on its axis once every twenty-four hours that gives us day and night, so it is this same turning of the earth which causes the moon to appear, or rise, as we are turned round far enough to see it, and later, causes it to disappear, or set, as we are turned still further around until we can no longer see it. If the moon stood still, as regards the earth, we would, in turning round every day on our axis, come into sight of the moon, or have moonrise, at the same time every day. As it is, the moon has moved on during each day a considerable distance in its course, so that we do not find it one day where we found it the day before, and must keep turning on round until we catch up with it, again. It requires, on the average, about 50 minutes each day, for us to move the extra distance necessary to enable us to catch up—in other words, the moon rises on the average, about 50 minutes later each day. This difference varies, however, on account of the varying inclination of the earth's orbit to our horizon at different times in the year, the difference in time of moonrise being sometimes as little as 17 minutes, and at other times as much as over 76 minutes. Just at this time, by the way, the difference is great, being about 70 minutes, or 1 hour and 10 minutes.

Now, I trust, you understand these changes of the moon and know what has become of the moon when we do not see it—no doubt, a puzzling matter to very many. You know, now, that the moon is always in her proper place, whether we see her or not. When so situated that she brightens our night, we have the best of evidence that she is with us, but she is none the less with us during what we call the 'dark of the moon,' though so situated that we may not see her. We can, however, as some of you may have noticed, even during this period occasionally see the moon showing faintly in the daytime, sometimes late in the forenoon or quite early in the afternoon, the sun's brightness not altogether hiding it at these times.

Possibly, it was ignorance of the fact that the moon is always in its place, whether we see it or not, and looks down upon our part of the earth, as upon other parts of it, during several hours of each day or night, the year around, that was at the foundation of much of the 'moonshine' of which I spoke a few minutes ago—the old superstitious and ridiculous notions. No doubt the changes of the moon—its appearance, as a new moon, its rapid increase and decrease—its 'waxing and waning,' as it is termed—and then its utter disappearance for a time was a puzzling matter, and is so yet, of course, to people not aware of the cause of all these changes; possibly, many may have entertained the idea, as some may, even to-day, that the new moon was an actual new moon each month, beginning as a narrow crescent strip and actually growing larger up to full moon, and then wasting away day by day, until it was all gone. But however this may be, the matter of the moon's changes, puzzling and mysterious as it was to those not aware of the cause of these changes, would furnish ground for all kinds of notions touching the effect of these changes upon our commonest earthly affairs. Since, though, the moon itself is always present and never changes, the changes we see being only the difference in the amount of its sunlighted surface which we are able to see at different times, it would seem that whatever effect, if any, the moon's changes could have would be due, not to the difference in the amount of light we receive from it at the different times, as this light, as you have learned, is simply the sunlight falling on the moon and reflected or thrown off again to us, but due, rather, to the varying direction of the moon's attraction as related to the attraction of the sun—the moon's attraction being in the same direction as that of the sun at new moon, in exactly the opposite direction at full moon, and more or less opposed to it at all other points in its monthly course, including the first and last quarters, or quadratures, where it is at a right angle to it.

It will surprise you, I am pretty sure, to be told that our earth plays the part of a moon to our moon, going through exactly the same changes, as it would be seen from the moon, that we here on the earth see taking place on the moon, with this difference, that at any time the appearance of one is exactly the opposite of that of the other. For instance, we see the moon to-night at nearly the first quarter point, but if we were on the moon we should see our earth at nearly last quarter. At the time of new moon, when the bright side of the moon is turned away from us and the dark side toward us so we cannot see it at all, the sunlighted or day side of the earth, as you can understand, will be turned fairly and fully toward the moon, and if then on the moon we should see a 'full earth,'—looking in general like our full moon, only being, of course, very much larger. So, when the moon has passed half way around us in her monthly journey and presents her whole sunlighted side to us as the full moon, our earth, you can again see, has its dark or night side turned to the moon, and to the moon there is a 'new earth,' and so on.

Yes, Bess, our earth shines just as the moon shines, by reflecting or throwing off again into space the light received from the sun. To us here upon it, the earth is only a great dark-colored globe, but viewed from the moon or from any of the planets we should see it shining just as these other bodies shine to us. The planets, as I think I told you the other night, are of themselves dark, like our own earth, and the light they show us as we see them at night is, like moonlight, the light of the sun reflected from them to us. The reason they appear only like stars, while the moon, which is so very, very much smaller than they are, appears so much larger, is all owing to the great difference between the distance from us of the moon, which is quite a near neighbor, as I have said, and of the planets which are so many millions of miles away. Viewed through the astronomers' great telescopes, however, these far-away planets are apparently brought so close that they do not appear as mere bright points like stars, but as round bright disks like the moon. Yes, our dull looking earth shines brightly by throwing back into space the sunshine it receives, and, if there are dwellers on the other planets, they see our earth—as we on the earth see them—shining, star-like, in the sky, surrounded by other stars.

Please move your head slightly, Ned, so I can get a good look at the moon—maybe I can give you a striking proof that the earth shines. Ah! I thought so—there's the proof staring you in the face. Just take a good look at the moon, and then tell me if you can see anything besides the bright crescent shaped part. Yes, that's what I mean, Ned—that large, round, dim thing, as you term it, filling up the hollow of the bright crescent and extending out beyond its points; I'm glad you all see it—though no doubt all of you have seen it before. Well, that is the other part of the side of the moon now turned toward us, but on which the sun is not shining—the remainder of the sunlighted side being turned away from us. As the sun is not shining upon the part which we can faintly see, how is it that this part is shining, at all?—shining enough for us to see it? Well, I'll explain the matter: The dim light with which this part of the moon is shining is received from our earth, being nothing less, indeed, than the very same moonlight which we are ourselves receiving from the bright part of the moon—which, in turn, is the sunlight which is now falling upon it while we have our backs to the sun, as we may say. Let us trace this light: First, it comes from the sun, of course; falling upon the moon, it is then reflected from it, into space, our earth receiving a part of it; then our earth itself reflects it into space, and the moon receives a part of it back again; then the moon again reflects it, and it is the light of this last reflection which we see coming from the dim part of the moon; so, you see, our earth shines, and it is its shining, or reflecting of the moonlight we are receiving, which is now dimly lighting up what would, otherwise, be at this time a dark part of the moon. If, then, our earth shines to this degree in the moonlight, you can well understand that it must shine very brightly indeed, as it reflects the direct and intense light of the sun to other worlds. Who knows but our earth is the brightest and most beautiful of the planets, outrivaling, as viewed from some other planet, even beautiful Venus herself!

I have not yet told you what the moon is like, further than to speak of its shape and size. Supposing, then, that we should take a part of our wonderful imaginary railroad trip over again, the eight months part of it, what would we find when we should reach the moon? Well, according to the best information the astronomers are able to give us, we should find a world very different from the one in which we are living. By the use of their great telescopes, the astronomers are able to apparently bring the moon close enough to appear as it would to our eyes at a distance of 125 or 150 miles from us—a distance small enough to enable them to determine some things in regard to it, but still too great to enable them to settle a number of very important points about which we would all like to have information; at the distance named, only the very largest objects can be seen, as you can well understand when you consider that we cannot see a man five miles off.

The astronomers tell us that the moon's surface presents a scene of great desolation. Great volcanoes have at some long-ago time been in eruption upon it, though not now, and everywhere are found the craters of these now extinct volcanoes. They form immense basins, as it were, or sunken plains, some of them 100 miles in diameter and very deep—some of the smaller ones being three or four miles deep, and the sides or walls of the old crater rising nearly straight to this height. In the center of these basins a conical peak rises, while masses of rock, in huge blocks, lie scattered about in them. Great mountain peaks also appear among them, many very lofty ones—some of them, indeed, exceeding in height the loftiest ones on our earth. There are, too, plains—or what appear to be such—like our prairies. There are other appearances, too, the nature of which is not understood. As judged by the appearance of the side we see, the moon is believed by the astronomers to be a dead world.

Many photographs of the moon, as apparently brought near us, have been taken by the astronomers, so that by examining these pictures we can see the moon very much as it appears to the astronomers themselves while viewing it through their telescopes. Fortunately, I happen to have, and so am able to show you, an engraving made from such a photograph—here it is. The photograph from which this was engraved is said to be the best ever taken. It was taken at the great Lick Observatory, at San Francisco, It shows the moon, as you notice, as it appears at first quarter—being a little larger than it appears to us in the sky, this evening, as the first quarter point for this month will not be reached, as I have already told you, until after midnight of to-morrow. Here you see the craters, looking right down into those that face fairly toward us, as do these here near the straight edge. Down at the bottom of some of those into which the sun is shining you can see the round, tapering peaks of which I told you. The black spot on the side and bottom of some of the craters is the shadow cast by the high, steep walls or sides, which shut out the sunlight from the depths of some of them, almost entirely.

The other half of the side of the moon facing us would be just here at the left, but is not to be seen because the sun is not shining upon it; it is in the dark, but is, of course, there just the same, and would appear had the picture been taken at the time of full moon, when the sun would have been shining on the whole side of the moon facing us. As it is, the sunshine extended at the time the picture was taken, over only as much of this side of the moon as we see in the picture. The edge of the bright part appears broken and ragged, you notice; the dark patches which give the edge this irregular shape are the shadows of great mountains which catch the sunlight, and so prevent it, for the time, from falling upon and lighting up the valleys or plains beyond them. As we view the moon with our unaided eyes, as we see it, now, through the window, we cannot, on account of its distance, notice these shadows, the edge appearing to be straight.

PHOTOGRAPH OF MOON AT FIRST QUARTER.

Taken at Lick Observatory, San Francisco, showing moon as it would appear to the naked eye at a distance of about 150 miles.

I should add, here, that we always see the same side of the moon,
the same side being always turned toward us. This is due to the fact
that the moon does not turn on its axis once in 24 hours, or some
such short period, as does the earth, but just once during the time in
which it revolves around the earth—nearly a month, you know. This
causes the same side to be always turned toward us, whereas, if it turned
on its axis in either a shorter or longer period, we would be able to see the
whole of it in the course of its revolutions around us. As it is, we never
have seen and never can see the other side of the moon, and what it is
like, or what may be there are matters about which we can never know
anything, whatever. We do, however, see a little more than half of
the moon, as, owing to two or three causes, we are able to see at one
time a little beyond the usual limit on one side, and at another time
about the same distance beyond the usual limit on the other side; so
that if we were to consider the moon as divided into 1,000 parts, we
can see, altogether, about 576 of these parts. Here is a picture made
to represent such a scene as it is supposed would be found could we
visit the moon.

What is on the other side is a mystery. The astronomers tell us
that they cannot discover anything like air or water on this side of the
moon; neither do they think it likely that there is any kind of life on
this side, though of this they cannot be certain; however, people, animals or plants, if there are any on this side, must be very different
from those of our earth in many respects, to enable them to live without air and water, if, as it appears, neither of these is to be found.
But as to the other side it may be different. It is heavier than this
side, the astronomers have discovered, and all the air and water which
the moon may have, if it has either, at all, is on that account collected
on the other side. If they are there—something which we will probably never know—that side of the moon may be inhabited like our
earth, and, like it, filled with life in many forms. But as to this we, of
course, really know nothing at all.

The question of whether or not the moon is inhabited, has long
been a most interesting one, and more than one wonderful story has
been set afloat to the effect that it has been discovered that it is inhabited. I recollect one which was printed in the newspapers far and
wide a few years ago. It was to the effect that a boy of about Ned's
age, living in California, was gifted with a remarkable pair of eyes,
with which he could plainly see people on the moon, their houses, etc.,
all of which he described very minutely. Though nothing but a great
hoax, the story was no doubt believed by many who read it.

Can't we make telescopes which will enable us to see people on
the moon, if there are any there? is a question, Miss Inquisitive,
which astronomers and telescope makers would be glad to answer—
yes, but it is one to which, for the present, at least, they are compelled
to answer—no. It is a most difficult piece of work to manufacture the

AN IDEAL LANDSCAPE ON THE MOON.

great curved pieces of glass called the *lenses*, used in telescopes, so as
to have them free from any imperfections, a very slight one of which
would make them unreliable and unfit for use; but even with every
lens in the telescope perfect, and all combined, of great power, we
should still fail of accomplishing the object sought. Astronomers
find that the currents of the air greatly affect their ability to see the
moon and other bodies far out in space through a telescope. Beyond
a certain point an increase in the power of a telescope to magnify or
enlarge distant objects is useless—indeed, worse than useless, as beyond that point an increased power instead of making objects more
distinct, only blurs them and blots them from the sight entirely. For
this reason, then, we are unable to use our great telescopes, as otherwise we might, so as to see the smallest objects on the moon, the
smallest now seen being those' not less than 300 to 600 feet in length
or diameter; you can see, then, how impossible it is for us to see objects so small as a man. Our telescopes no doubt would do their part
of the work, but until the interference of the air is overcome, which
may never be, they will be unable to aid us beyond the present limit.

In connection with this question of whether or not the moon is
inhabited, I have seen it stated, recently, that the King of Wurtem-
berg is about to try a new method of discovery. He will have taken
a number of the best photographs of the moon it is possible to secure,
and will then have these photographs enlarged 100,000 times, which
operation will, it is hoped, be so successful that the smallest objects
on the moon will be made plainly apparent, and all questions be thus
finally answered."

XI.

ECLIPSES.

"And, now, we will take up a matter of which I spoke last night and
of which I promised to tell you more to-night, a matter in which the
moon plays a most important part—eclipses.

An eclipse may be defined as the hiding, or covering over, of any
body by the coming between us and it of some other body. An eclipse
of the sun, as I briefly stated, last night, is caused by the moon coming,
in the course of its monthly journey, exactly between us and the sun,
while an eclipse of the moon—for the moon itself is also often eclipsed—is
caused by the earth coming exactly between the sun and the moon.
I will try to explain to you the matters of eclipses of both sun and moon,
so you will be able to understand them.

You have already seen how the moon in the course of its monthly
journey comes in between the sun and earth, at the time of new moon,

though usually passing a little higher or a little lower than the sun, and not exactly between it and the earth; but occasionally—not less than two, or more than five, times a year—it does thus come directly in front of the sun, and we have then an eclipse of the sun. If the path of the moon around the earth lay in the same plane—or, as I may put it for you, if it agreed exactly in direction with the path of the earth around the sun, the moon would then come thus directly between us and the sun each time it circles around us, and we should have an eclipse every time we have new moon, about once a month, you see. But the all-wise Creator in appointing the moon its path caused it to be slightly inclined or 'tipped' to the earth's path, so that it is partly above and partly below the path of the earth, and it is owing to this fact that the moon passes the sun, usually either a little higher or lower than it is, and thus avoids eclipsing it every time it goes around the earth. The moon's path lying thus partly above and partly below the earth's path, the moon in following it round and round, monthly, will cross the earth's path twice—once in going below, and once in coming again above, the earth's path. These crossing points are called *nodes*, the one where the moon crosses our path in passing below it being called the *descending node*, and the other, where it crosses again in passing above it, the *ascending node*. It is only when the moon is just at or very near one of these crossing points or nodes, at the time it comes in between us and the sun, at new moon, that it comes directly between us and the sun, instead of passing above or below it, as it usually does.

As the moon thus comes fairly in front of the sun, with its dark side, of course, toward us, its round dark body is seen moving across the sun's face, sometimes covering up the whole sun in the course of its passage—in which case the eclipse is called a *total* one—or perhaps covering only a larger or smaller portion of the sun—in which case it is called a *partial* eclipse. As the moon moves from west to east, it is first seen on the western edge, or *limb*, as it is called, of the sun, and covering more and more of the sun as it moves forward, until it reaches the eastern edge and begins to pass off—the western side of the sun re-appearing as the moon passes on eastward, until, the moon having entirely passed by, we see the whole sun, again, as before.

As the moon is so much smaller than the earth, and is at such a distance from it, it cannot thus hide the sun from the whole side of the earth, but only from a part of it, the sun shining past it upon all the other parts, as before—there being no eclipse in these parts. Just the belt or strip of the earth on which the shadow cast by the moon falls sees the eclipse, while to those places outside of this strip nothing unusual occurs, the moon, to these places, passing, as usual, either above or below the sun. The strip of the earth's surface from which the sunlight is entirely cut off by the moon is quite narrow, averaging only about 140 miles, but being sometimes wider, sometimes narrower, than this, according as the moon happens to be at its least or greatest distance from the earth at the time of the eclipse. But though it is thus narrow, it is in a sense quite long—thousands of miles, indeed—as the turning of the earth on its axis is every instant bringing a new part of its surface into the shadow, while, of course, carrying a corresponding part out again on the farther side. But outside of the strip of deepest shadow, where the eclipse is total, the sun being entirely covered, there is, on each side, a wider strip in which the shadow is less deep, only a part of the sun being covered—the eclipse in these strips being only partial. Beyond these strips of lighter shadow the sun is shining as usual, the moon, as I have said, being too small to cut off the light from these other parts.

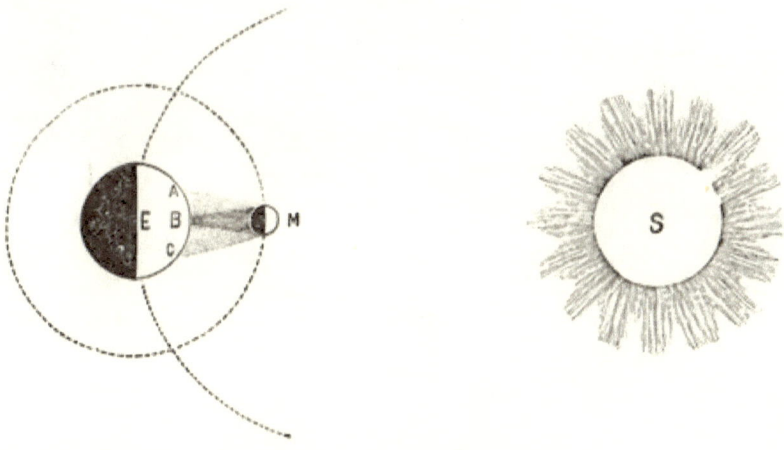

AN ECLIPSE OF THE SUN.

To persons at B, the eclipse will be total, the sun being entirely hidden by the moon; to persons at A, there will be a partial eclipse, the *lower* part of sun being hidden, and to persons at C, a partial eclipse, the *upper* part of sun being hidden.

Here—I will draw a picture, representing an eclipse. Here is the sun, here the earth, and here between the two is the moon. The sun being larger than the moon, it will cause the round shadow thrown by the moon in coming between it and the earth to run to a point toward the earth—thus. When the moon is farthest from the earth, the shadow may thus come to a point before reaching the earth, but when nearer, the shadow reaches the earth as I have shown, the width of the shadow when it reaches the earth depending, as I stated a moment ago, upon the distance of the moon at the time. Now, as the earth turns on its axis and the moon, too, moves forward, a long strip of the earth's surface, as I have already said, is brought into this shadow, and has a total eclipse. Above and below this dark shadow is the lighter shadow—so—covering the part of the earth from which only a

part of the sun is hidden, or, in other words, in which there is a partial eclipse. There was, as I told you last night, a total eclipse of the
sun on last Sunday, but the moon's position was such that its shadow

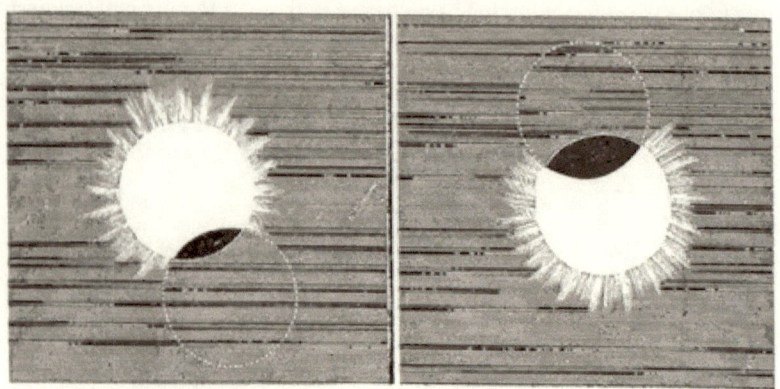

Moon hiding lower limb of sun.   Moon hiding upper limb of sun.

PARTIAL ECLIPSES.

did not reach to us. This strip or deep dark part of the shadow extended from South America across the ocean to Africa, and if we had
been within this strip, whether on the land or on a vessel on the ocean,

PATH OF TOTAL ECLIPSE OF DECEMBER 22, 1889.

the sun would have been entirely hidden from us by the moon; while
if we had been within the reach of the lighter part of the shadow,
north or south of the very dark strip, we should have seen the moon

pass over a part of the sun—the lower part if we had been north of the darkest strip, the upper part if we had been south of it; as it was, being entirely out of reach of the moon's shadow, we saw no eclipse—there was nothing of an unusual nature. This picture I am drawing will show the course of the total eclipse of last Sunday, as represented by this black strip.

Although the moon, in the case of a total eclipse, may be several hours in passing across the sun, the time during which it actually entirely covers it in its passage, viewed from any one point, is very short, only three or four minutes, as the moon is traveling at more than a 38-mile a minute rate. It is during this brief space—the time of *totality*, as it is termed—that the mysterious and magnificent appearance of which I spoke last night, the sun's corona, is to be seen.

Although, on account of distance, the moon seems to move slowly across the sun, it is traveling, as I have just stated, with great speed .

3. Passing off.　　　　　2. Total.　　　　　1. Beginning.

TOTAL ECLIPSE OF THE SUN.

—as would be readily apparent could we watch, from some elevated position, the moon's shadow on the earth sweeping along, as a great black spot, across mountains, valleys, rivers, or the great ocean. Astronomers and others who have, from some mountain top, been able to see 50 or 100 miles or more of its course, describe its approach as a most impressive sight—to some of them even a terrifying one—as it comes swiftly sweeping toward them or past them like some great black monster racing across the land, climbing mountains and leaping rivers as they come in its course.

The circumstances attending an eclipse are, of course, peculiar—it is the darkness of early night coming upon us perhaps at midday. We first see the round edge of the moon on the western edge of the sun, and see it minute after minute creeping further across, hiding more and more of the bright sun, until a strange and ghastly twilight, as it were, comes upon us, causing flowers to close, while birds and animals, mistaking it for nightfall, seek their places of nightly rest. As

the moon advances farther, the darkness increases until the stars appear and the air becomes chill and damp as at night. Finally, the
whole sun is hidden behind the moon—and now, for a little time, the
sun's corona may be seen streaming off into space. The moon moving
steadily on, begins to uncover the part of the sun first hidden, more
and more of the sun coming again into view, at the same rate at which
it disappeared, and the light increasing again until, the moon now well
past, the flowers open again, the birds begin to'sing and the chickens
to crow, as though for the dawning of another day,—and we may fancy
their astonishment at the shortness of the night! If the grass is ex-
amined, dew may be found upon it, as in the morning, the temperature
of the air having been lowered so much during the time the sunshine
has been cut off. Very likely you will at some time witness such an
eclipse, as I have been permitted to do.

When an eclipse occurs at the time of the moon's greatest distance

AN ANNULAR ECLIPSE,

from the earth, the whole face of the sun is not hidden by it, but a
ring of the bright sun is left uncovered all around the moon's dark
body, part of this ring sometimes appearing to be separated into a
number of parts, looking like a string of beads, being called Bailey's
Beads, in honor of their discoverer. Such an eclipse—which of course
is nearly a total one—is called an *annular* one—not annual, mind—the
word annular meaning ring-like, this name being given it on account
of the ring of the sun appearing around the moon.

But the moon itself is often eclipsed, as I have already told you.
An eclipse of the moon is caused by the earth cutting off the moon's
sunshine, just as we have seen the moon cut off the earth's sunshine. It always occurs, of course, at the time of full moon, when the
earth is between the sun and moon—not directly between them, usually,
as you know, but only occasionally, at which times we have the eclipse.
If the paths of the earth and the moon agreed, as before explained, we
would have an eclipse of the moon at every time of full moon, as we

would have an eclipse of the sun at every new moon. But for the same reason that the moon can come directly between us and the sun only occasionally, the earth is brought, in the course of the moon's journeys around it, fairly between it and the sun only occasionally. Of course, we see an eclipse of the moon at night, and the eclipse may be total or partial according as the moon's position brings it fully into the shadow cast by the earth into space, or brings only a part of it into the shadow. Here—*I* will make another picture to show you an eclipse of the moon. Here is the sun, here the earth, this dark part is the shadow thrown by the earth into space, and here, next, is the moon's path around the sun. Now, when the moon in journeying around the earth gets into a position which places it directly behind the earth from the sun there falls upon it, not the sunshine, but the dark shadow

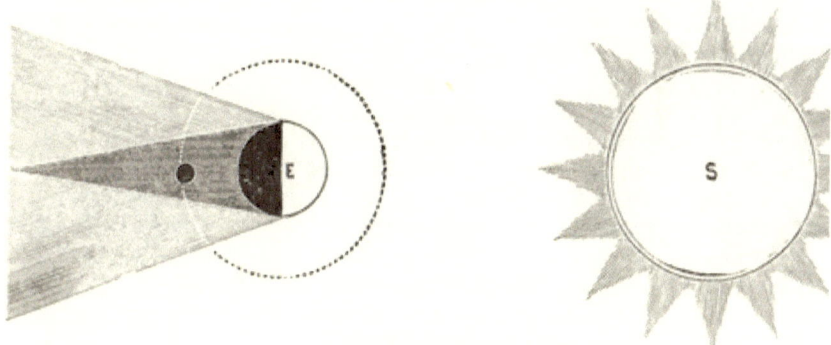

ECLIPSE OF THE MOON.

of our earth—which we see creeping across it, as we see the moon itself creeping across the sun, at the time of a sun eclipse.

There will be three eclipses in the coming year, 1890,—two of the sun and one of the moon; none of them, however, can be seen in our country—so you will have to wait awhile to see one. Asia, Africa and Australia are the countries from which these eclipses are to be seen, I may state. There will, also, be what is termed a *lunar appulse*.

I must say a few words about the tides before we close our talk on the moon. Probably all of you have read or heard of the tides, and those of you who have visited the sea-shore have seen them, but perhaps none of you know anything about their cause. Twice a day, or every twelve hours—really a little more than this, as it occurs a little later each day—the waters of the ocean rise and fall. For about six hours the waves roll in, and the water rises along the coast, and up in the bays and rivers for a long distance from the coast, to a height of several feet, and then ebbs or falls again, for about the same length of time; then it again rises for another six hours, to be followed again by another similar period of ebbing—and this rising and falling goes on continually. The cause of this ceaseless movement which we call the tides is, mainly, the attraction of the moon, the sun, however, having something to do with the matter by his attraction, so that we have a *moon tide* and a *solar tide*, though the moon tide is the principal one.

The moon's attraction, which, on account of its comparative nearness to the earth, is very great, causes the water on the side of the earth facing it, as the earth revolves, to be lifted or heaped up toward it in a wave which follows the moon in its course; at the same time, the earth is being drawn toward the moon, and, in a measure, drawn away from the water on the opposite side, which is thus left heaped up. The sun's influence upon the water, I shall state, is not equal to quite half that of the moon. When the sun and moon act together, as at new moon or full moon, the highest tide, called *spring tide* is produced; when the moon is at first or third quarter, they are pulling against each other, as it were, and we have the lowest or *neap tide*—the moon, at all times, producing the principal effects in the matter of the tides.

Now, I have given you, in a general way, the principal facts in connection with the subject of the moon, and I will—Oh, dear me! yes; I did nearly forget that poor fellow, though it is evident, Miss Inquisitive, you had no intention of allowing him to be forgotten. As to this 'Man in the Moon,' then, I must confess that I have not the pleasure and honor of numbering him in my list of acquaintances. I have heard of him, of course, ever since I was a bit of boy like Willie here, and I have seen all kinds of queer portraits of his face in all kinds of pictures of the crescent moon and full moon, but I have never seen him—nor has any one else, so far as I have been able to learn, although he has been talked about for ever so many years. Indeed, it's my notion—mind I tell it to you in strict confidence, and you must never say I told you so—but it is my notion that there neither is, nor ever was, such a person as the 'Man in the Moon', and that all talk about him is nothing but 'moonshine.'"

XII.

STARS AND NEBULÆ.

"Now, we have finished our talk about the moon, but as it is not yet late, I think I will say a few words about the stars, as they present so wonderfully interesting a field for thought and study that I should be leaving my astronomical talks unfinished did I not give the stars more particular mention than I have yet given them.

I have already told you that the astronomers inform us that each of the far-off stars we see, with the millions upon millions more which they can see by the aid of their great telescopes, is a great sun, like our own, and probably surrounded by a number of planets or worlds, like our own and the others of our system. Each star—or sun as we are to believe it to be—with its worlds, if what we may suppose is correct, forms a system like ours, each perhaps separated from the others as widely as ours from any of them, by distances of not millions but trillions of miles!—distances utterly inconceivable. What must be the immensity of space, then, to contain to us unnumbered millions of systems like our own, each separated from the other by a distance inconceivably great!—and not only this, but affording room for all of these systems, our own included, to circle, in vast orbits, about some far-away central point! Our own sun, with its whole system of worlds, is sweeping through space around this far-off center, wherever and whatever it may be, at the rate of 8 miles per second, and even at this rate it will be probably a million years in completing its wonderful circuit!—just how long has not yet been determined. It has been estimated, however, that a certain well-known and comparatively near star, or sun, will be 185,000 years in making the journey! another one 350,000 years! while the faintly seen ones will be millions of years in making the circuit! Amazing the power, amazing the wisdom, which has created and which thus sustains and directs this countless host!

The far-distant center around which all the systems are thus circling is believed to be a point lying in the constellation called Hercules. Just what this one great central point of influence may be is not known. It is a beautiful and impressive thought—and may it not be a truthful one?—of Bishop Warren, that it may be the Eternal City of GOD, where reigns the King and Lord of all, the countless millions of worlds being the distant provinces of His material kingdom, all moving in His sight and receiving power from a mind that never wearies.

Although all the stars (suns) are thus in motion, so far away are they that we never see them moving—nor can we detect more than the slightest change in position, in the case of some of them, in a life-time, so far away are they! How far? That is a hard question to answer, as the astronomers themselves will tell you. The method by which the astronomers seek to measure the distances of these far-off bodies I shall not try to explain to you now, but I will state that it is a most difficult and delicate matter to measure the distance of even the nearest ones. When I say nearest, I do not at all mean *near*, as you will discover in a moment. Distances in space, even between the bod-ies making up our own system, are amazing, as you are well aware; but when we come to consider distances as related to the stars our amazement is increased a hundredfold. For instance, we are told that the distance of the nearest star, called Alpha Centauri, is 21,000,-000,000,000 miles! That, remember, is the distance of the *nearest* one, one that we can see with our unaided eyes. What, then, must be the distance of those very, very far-away ones that can be but very faintly seen even through the most powerful telescopes! So distant are the stars that their light, though traveling at the wonderful speed of 186,000 miles per second, is years in reaching us. The light from Alpha Centauri, the nearest star, requires about 3½ years to reach us; that from Polaris nearly 50 years, and that from the far, far-away stars, hundreds and even many thousands of years! I may add, here, that we get a little heat, as well as light, from the stars—they are blazing suns, you know.

As the stars are thus all in motion, it will come to pass in the course of many thousands of years that their positions will be so changed that the sky will present quite a different appearance from that presented in our time. Stars and groups of stars forming well-known shapes that are familiar to us now in the sky, will be in far dif-ferent positions in the distant future. The stars, I should tell you, are divided up into great groups called *constellations*, each of which covers a considerable part of the sky and includes quite a number of stars. These constellations are again divided up into various smaller groups which have received names, those of a few being given to them from their resemblance to things whose names they bear, but most of them bearing names of animals and of heathen heroes, warriors, hunters, etc., given them thousands of years ago by the ancient Greeks. Be-sides this grouping, the stars, to the number of 300,000 or more, have been named or numbered, and their positions marked on charts, so that the astronomer can quickly find on his chart or in the sky any star that he may want to observe. While only the astronomer with his star chart or map and his great telescope is able to find the most of these named stars, we may, by a little hard study and a little help from some one already familiar with them, be able to point out the various constellations and many of the smaller groups, and to point out and name many of the most familiar stars. For instance, there is Polaris or the ' Pole Star,' so called because of its position in

the northern sky, apparently just above the north pole, and which, because of its position thus always in the north, has guided to safety
thousands lost upon land and sea, by silently but plainly telling them
that toward it is north, knowing which, they could then tell with certainty which way was
south or east or west,
and so turn their course
toward home or haven.
Then there is Sirius, the
'Dog Star,' the brightest
in the sky and one about
which boys and girls
should be especially in-
terested, as it is during
the time this beautiful
star is particularly no-
ticeable in the sky that
fearful mothers caution
them about the 'dog-
days.' Then there are the
groups to study—ever so
many of them. There is
Cassiopeia's Chair, the
Dippers, the—ah, yes!
you boys all know the
two Dippers, it seems;
was there ever a boy who
didn't know the Dippers,
though he knew nothing
else among the stars?
And, by the way, speak-
ing of the Dipper reminds
me of the matter about
which I had started out
to tell you when I wan-
dered off among all the
constellations.

I began to tell you
about the changes which
will occur in the appear-
ance of the sky, in the
course of thousands of years, by the movements of the far-off stars—
how they will change positions, the old familiar groups being broken up
and new ones formed. You are to always remember, however, that although the stars of any of these groups seem close together, they are actually separated by millions upon millions of miles, so that if we should be

able to go to any one of them, we should find the others appearing still
as far distant as they did from the earth.   As to the changes in these
groups, we shall never be able to notice them in our brief lifetime, nor
will they appear much changed generations hence; but the stars
are all in swiftest motion, flying through space, and although their distance is so great that from century to century the changes caused by
their movements are scarcely to be noticed, yet the time will some day
come when these slowly growing changes will have entirely altered the
appearance of the starry heavens.   The same movements have been
going on, of course, in the past as they are now going on, and will continue to go on forever.   For instance, one of the groups which you
boys all seem to know so well, the Great Dipper, has not always had
its present form, nor will it always keep it.   I have some pictures here
which will show the changes which have taken place, and which will
take place, in this group.   The first one, here, shows the positions of
the stars of the present Dipper group as they appeared away back
100,000 years ago,—there is no dipper shape there at all, you see.   But
they have changed their positions since that time, and we now have,
as we long have had and will have, the familiar form of the Dipper.
These little arrows in the picture show the direction in which each
star has been moving from its position of 100,000 years ago, and which
movement has brought them into their present positions so that they
form the present dipper-shaped group in the sky, as we have it in this
second picture.   But they are still moving onward, though we do not
notice the movement, these little arrows in this second picture showing
in which direction each is now traveling.   Inside another 100,000 years
they will have long lost, again, their present dipper-like form, and will
appear as in this third picture—which looks not the least bit like a dipper.
And so with all the other stars we see, each and every one is in motion,
and all the groups are slowly but surely being changed.

Here—I'll make a picture showing some of the stars, groups and
constellations of which I have just spoken—a part of those that make
up what are called the *northern circumpolar constellations*, that is,
those surrounding the north pole of the heavens as marked, very nearly,
by Polaris, or the Pole Star or North Star as it is commonly called.
There—we have a picture of these stars and groups as they appear at
this moment;* come to this north window, all of you, and I'll point out
the real stars and groups, as they are shown here in my picture.

You all know the Big Dipper, over here at the right, so we will
begin with it.   It forms a part of the constellation known as *Ursa
Major* or the *Great Bear*, to which constellation belong, also, many of
the other stars that you see around the Dipper and others that we
cannot see to-night—there being, in all, 138 stars in this constellation
which may be seen by our unaided eyes on a favorable night.   The

---

*The positions of these constellations here presented corresponds to their actual
positions at nine o'clock on the night of December 21 of each year.

Dipper itself is made up of seven stars, as you know, and which I have connected with dotted lines in our picture. Those two fine stars forming the end of the Dipper next to the handle are called the 'Pointers', for the reason that, taken together, they always point in the direction of Polaris, or the North Star, and thus enable one to find that star.—Aha! some of you have taken my hint and found the North Star for yourselves—that bright one, there, Willie. The 'Pointers', you can readily understand, are of perhaps equal value to the North Star

itself, to a lost person who is not sufficiently familiar with the stars to find the North Star without their friendly assistance.

The North Star, as you now know it and can hereafter find it, is one of the seven which make up the Little Dipper, and forms the end of the handle. This group forming the Little Dipper belongs to a constellation known as *Ursa Minor* or the *Little Bear*, which contains, in all, 24 stars, only a few of which, besides those in the Little Dipper itself, can be seen to-night.

That bright star out to the right of the cup part of the Little Dipper is called *Thuban*. This star, astronomers tell us, was the North or Pole Star 4,000 years ago,—so Polaris has not always held its present distinguished position; nor will it, indeed, always retain that position, as the astronomers further tell us that, 12,000 years from this time, that bright star yonder, in a little constellation called Lyra,* will be the pole star. Polaris is now, I may add, about 1½ degrees from the true polar position.

Up yonder, above and to the left of the Little Dipper, is the constellation known as *Cassiopeia*. Cassiopeia was a queen, according to the old Greek mythology—what we term mythology being the system of most entertaining but most ridiculous fables believed in by the ancients, and which, indeed, formed their religion. There are to be seen, on a favorable night, 55 stars in this constellation. The most striking ones are the seven which form *Cassiopeia's Chair*, as it is termed—the chair on which this fabled queen was supposed to sit. By the dotted lines connecting these seven stars, in the picture, you can better catch the chair-shaped arrangement of the stars in this group—a very familiar one, by the way.

The three groups I have pointed out are familiar ones to nearly everybody, although their names, as, also, the names of some of the principal stars, as I have given them to you, are familiar to but comparatively few. Around and between these groups and constellations are other constellations, large and small, embracing all the stars we can see. Below Cassiopeia is the constellation called *Cepheus*—Cepheus, according to mythology, being a king and Cassiopeia's husband. Above her is the constellation called *Perseus*—Perseus being the son-in-law of Cassiopeia. Yonder, above the Little Dipper, is the constellation called the *Giraffe*, and yonder, again, one called the *Lynx*. Beginning with that group of large, bright stars below and a little to the left of the Little Dipper, there is a great constellation called *Draco*, or the *Dragon*, which stretches away up between the two Bears or Dippers, taking in the star Thuban, which I pointed out a moment ago. And so with all the stars, besides the few we can see from this window—they are thus divided into constellations, and there are many most beautiful and striking groups like the three I have pointed out to you. Some night, when it is the 'dark of the moon' and more stars can be seen, we will go out on the lawn and I will point out many more constellations, groups and stars, and also the planets that may be then visible. As the earth moves on in her course around the sun, we will, of course, see different stars and constellations at different seasons, some being seen only during summer nights, others in winter, and so on. The ones we are now looking at, however—those surrounding the pole—can be seen every night in the year, though the constant changing of the earth's position apparently changes their position as seen at different seasons. The turning of the earth on its axis, too, causes

*The constellation Lyra is not shown in the illustration; it lies, however, a little outside the circle, at the lower, left hand part, about opposite the little group of three bright stars.

them all to apparently circle around the North Star daily—or nightly, if you choose to put it that way—and if we shall look at them an hour later we will notice this apparent change, the Big Dipper being higher, Cassiopeia lower, and so on.

With a good telescope we are enabled to see many wonderful things unseen to our unaided eyes. What appears to our eyes as a single star may, through a telescope, appear as a double star, or a triple one, or one of even more parts. By a double star you are not to understand that there are two stars side by side, close together,— on the contrary they are millions of miles apart; but they are related to each other, however, though thus widely separated, both revolving about a common center, and the same is true of triple stars, or those made up of still more parts.

While most of the stars shine with a soft white light like our own sunlight—they are suns, too, you know—there are others that give us colored light—red, green, yellow, etc., these colors probably being caused by some element contained in the glowing suns. The presence of these colored stars adds to the wondrous beauty of the starry heavens as seen through the telescope.

Then there are stars which, though never having been seen before, suddenly blaze out in the sky. Some of these soon disappear again, while others remain. Then, again, stars which had before been seen, have now entirely disappeared. The reasons for all these strange happenings can only be guessed at.

According to the astronomers, suns and worlds are born, grow old and die, very much as do men, only the life of a sun or world is counted by millions upon millions of years. The countless millions of suns and worlds which throng the vast universe are not all of the same age. Some, we are told, are very old and even now dead, and others far advanced toward that end; others, again, like our own sun and our own world, are but comparatively old, and are yet full of life and energy; others still are comparatively young—although youth in these cases may mean millions of years. The difference in the color of the stars, I should add, in connection with this subject, is thought to be very largely, if not entirely, due to the difference in the ages of the stars or suns—the younger ones, being in the most intensely heated state, showing colors different from those that are more and more old, and consequently in a less and less heated condition. The plan or method by which GOD has created—and may still be creating—suns and systems has long been a matter for inquiry among astronomers, and theories embracing some wonderful operations and changes have been suggested touching the matter. Of these theories, however, you can learn more when you are older. Possibly worlds are still being created.

You all have seen the Milky Way—that great path of soft white light crossing the sky. To our eyes it is nothing but a soft, hazy belt, but through a powerful telescope we behold it—wonder of wonders!—

a great host of stars (suns), millions upon millions of them! Though separated each from each by immense distances, they appear to be close together, and so far away are they that they appear only as the hazy Milky Way to our unaided sight. There are, we are told, 18,000,000 stars (suns) in the Milky Way, and if each has its system of worlds like ours, what a multitude of worlds are in this great cluster, or zone, alone! The depth, alone, of this immense zone of stars, as given us by Herschel, the great astronomer, is astounding. With his great telescope he pierced the depths of this region of stars, and, as the result of his investigations, has estimated that its depth is such that there are in the distance across as many as 500 stars (suns), one behind the other, and each separated from the other by a distance as great as that of our earth from the nearest star! What immensity of space does this imply!—yet it is but a little part of it, after all. Our own sun, with our earth and the other bodies of our system, is a part of the Milky Way, I may add. Our great sun is simply a star, as viewed from any of the far-distant suns or planets of any of these other systems; while our own world and the other planets of our system are probably not seen from any of them—only our sun can be seen. The Milky Way stretches across the sky in the shape of a great, reclining letter ◁, our sun and its system of worlds occupying a position about where the streams, as we may call them, of suns branch out—a central position, in a sense.

Mitchel, the astronomer, after supposing that we have flown from our earth to one of the worlds belonging to the system of one of the stars (suns) in the Milky Way, says, in the course of one of his lectures:—'We have reached a new system of worlds revolving about another sun, and from this remote point we expect to see a new heaven as well as a new earth on which we stand. But no.—Lift up your eyes, and lo! the old familiar constellations are all there. * * All is unchanged, and the mighty distance over which we have journeyed is but the thousandth part of the entire diameter of this grand cluster of suns and systems; and although we have swept from our sun to the nearest fixed star, and have traveled a distance which light itself cannot traverse in less than ten years, yet the change wrought by this mighty journey, in the appearance of the heavens, is no greater than would be produced in the relative positions of persons composing this audience to a person near its center who should change his seat with his immediate neighbor!' Is this not wonderful?

But beyond the host of blazing suns and rushing planets which compose the Milky Way—what? Peering through our telescopes into the depths far, far beyond these suns and systems, we see great numbers of what seem to be patches of faint, hazy light. We bring to bear upon one of these inconceivably distant patches of light a telescope of greater power, and lo! like the hazy Milky Way itself this patch of light appears to our astonished eyes another countless multitude of blazing suns. All that we have already seen again repeated!—and our astronomer again breaks forth : 'We have reached the clustering of ten millions of stars. Look to the right, there is no limit;—look to the left, there is no end ! Above, below, suns rise upon suns, and systems upon systems, in endless and im-measurable perspective. Here is a new universe, as magnificent, as glorious as our own,—a new Milky Way whose vast diameter the flashing light would not cross in a thousand years !' And then he adds, 'Nor is this a solitary object. Go out on a clear, cold winter night and reckon the stars which strew the heavens, and count their num-ber, and for every single orb thus visible to the naked eye the telescope reveals a *universe*, far sunk in the depths of space, and scattered with

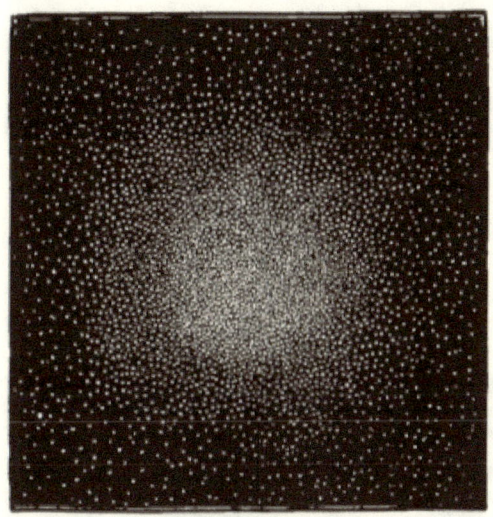

STAR CLUSTER.

vast profusion over the entire surface of the heavens. Some of these blaze with countless stars, while others, occupying the confines of visible space, but dimly stain the blue of the sky, just perceptible with the most powerful means man can summon to the aid of his vision !'

These far-distant patches of light are called *clusters* and *nebulæ*. The clusters are those which, as I have just described, have been dis-covered by the use of powerful telescopes, to be stars (suns) in count-less numbers! There are a great many of these clusters, and others are being added to the list from what were formerly supposed to be nebulæ. The nebulæ, I should state, are those of the far-away patches of light which do not prove to be star clusters, but instead are known to be great masses of gas of some kind. The nebulæ are very numer-ous, and new ones are being found. Some of these, however, may prove, by the use of yet more powerful telescopes, to be other star clusters, but many are known to be merely masses of gaseous matter. As to their source and purpose we can only guess. Some of them are of strange and beautiful shape, and have received names, in many

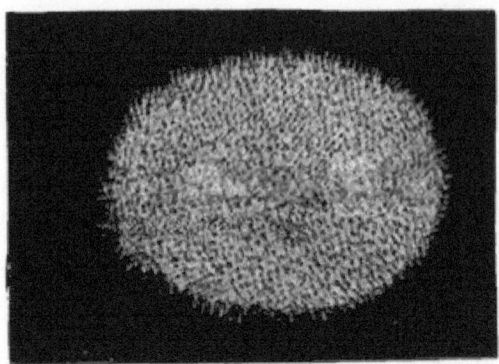

RING NEBULA.

cases, which express the fact of their resemblance to some familiar object—the resemblance being sometimes very close; for instance, we have the Crab, Horn, Spiral, Dumb-bell, Ring, and other nebulæ. Here are pictures of two nebulæ. There are about 8,000 known nebulæ.

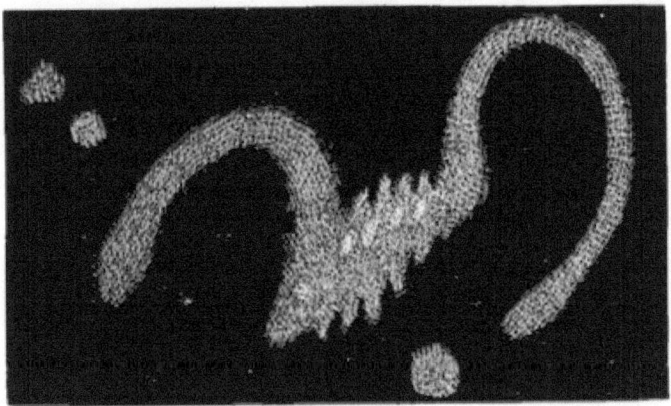

HORN NEBULA.

And, now, we have gone as far as we can—as far as the most pow-erful telescopes yet made can reach. What lies beyond we cannot tell, though having gone so far, we very naturally long to go yet farther in beholding the mysteries of GOD's great universe. In closing our talks, then, I cannot do so more fittingly than by repeating the language of what we may term the dream of the German poet, Richter,—a dream, yet embodying a wonderful, a glorious truth:—

'GOD called up from dreams a man into the vestibule of heaven, saying, "Come thou hither and see the glory of my house." And to the servants that stood around his throne He said, "Take him, and undress him from his robes of flesh; cleanse his vision, and put a new breath into his nostrils; only touch not with any change his human heart—the heart that weeps and trembles." It was done; and, with a mighty angel for his guide, the man stood ready for his infinite voyage; and from the terraces of heaven, without sound or farewell, at once they wheeled away into endless space. Sometimes with the solemn flight of angel wing they fled through Zaarrahs of darkness, through wildernesses of death, that divided the worlds of life; sometimes they swept over frontiers that were quickening under prophetic motions from GOD. Then, from a distance that is counted only in heaven, light dawned for a time through a sleepy film; by unutterable pace the light swept to them, they by unutterable pace to the light. In a moment the rushing of planets was upon them; in a moment the blazing of suns was around them.

Then came eternities of twilight, that revealed but were not revealed. On the right and on the left towered mighty constellations, that by self-repetitions and answers from afar, that by counter-positions built up triumphal gates whose architraves, whose archways—horizontal, upright—rested, rose, at altitude by spans that seemed ghostly from infinitude. Without measure were the architraves, past number were the archways, beyond memory the gates. Within were stairs that scaled the eternities below; above was below—below was above, to the man stripped of gravitating body; depth was swallowed up in height insurmountable, height was swallowed up in depth unfathomable. Suddenly, as thus they rode from infinite to infinite, suddenly, as thus they tilted over abysmal worlds, a mighty cry arose—that systems more mysterious, that worlds more billowy,—other heights and other depths,—were coming, were nearing, were at hand!

Then the man sighed and stopped, shuddered and wept. His overladened heart uttered itself in tears; and he said—"Angel, I will go no farther. For the spirit of man acheth with this infinity. Insufferable is the glory of GOD. Let me lie down in the grave and hide me from the persecution of the infinite; for end, I see, there is none!" And from all the listening stars that shone around issued a choral voice, "The man speaks truly: end there is none that ever yet we heard of." "End is there none?" the angel solemnly demanded: "is there indeed no end?—and is this the sorrow that kills you?" But no voice answered, that he might answer himself. Then the angel threw up his glorious hands to the heaven of heavens, saying, "End there is none to the universe of GOD. Lo, also, there is no beginning!"'

Good night."

APPENDIX.

TABLE OF ELEMENTS OF THE SOLAR SYSTEM. (Prof. Lewis Swift.)

	Diameter in miles.	Mean distance from sun in miles.	Velocity in orbit per second in miles.	Length of days.			Length of year in earth-days or years.	Number of moons.
				Hrs.	Min.	Sec.		
Sun......	870,000	......	......	......		......	......	......
Mercury ...	3,000	36,000,000	$29\frac{1}{2}$	24	5	(?)	$87\frac{97}{100}$ days	None
Venus......	7,700	68,000,000	$21\frac{9}{10}$	23	21	(?)	$224\frac{70}{100}$ days	None
Earth......	7,918	92,500,000	$18\frac{1}{10}$	23	56	$4\frac{1}{100}$	$365\frac{26}{100}$ days	1
Mars......	4,250	142,000,000	15	24	37	$22\frac{7}{10}$	$686\frac{98}{100}$ days	2
Asteroids..	......	250,000,000	......	......		......	......	......
Jupiter......	86,000	484,000,000	8	9	55	20	$11\frac{86}{100}$ years	4
Saturn .	71,000	886,000,000	$5\frac{6}{10}$	10	14	0	$29\frac{46}{100}$ years	8
Uranus...	33,000	1,780,000,000	4	Unknown.			$84\frac{2}{100}$ years	4
Neptune ...	37,000	2,800,000,000	$3\frac{6}{10}$	Unknown.			$164\frac{78}{100}$ years	1
Moon	2,160	238,000 Mean distance from earth.	About $\frac{6}{10}$	......		......	......	......

Period of Sun's axial rotation—25½ days.
Period of Moon's axial rotation—sidereal, 27⅓ days; synodic, 29½ days.
Number of Asteroids discovered to September 1, 1889—287.
Number of known periodic comets—20.
Number of known nebulæ—8,000.
Distance of nearest star, Alpha Centauri,—21,000,000,000,000 miles.

List of Refracting Telescopes in the United States, of a diameter of 11 inches, and larger. Those marked * are in process of construction.

(This list—by Prof. Lewis Swift—is the most perfect extant.)

Observatory.	*Diameter in Inches.*
Lick (1) Mt. Hamilton, Cal.	36
*Yale College, New Haven, Conn.	28
Naval, Washington, D. C.	26
University of Virginia, Charlottesville.	26
*Harvard College (Photographic, 1), Cambridge, Mass.	24
Princeton College, Princeton, N. J.	23
*Chamberlain, Denver, Colo.	20
Dearborn, Evanston, Ill.	18½
Warner, Rochester, N. Y.	16
*Carlton College, Northfield, Minn.	16
Washburn, Madison, Wis.	15½
Harvard University (2), Cambridge, Mass.	15
Litchfield, Clinton, N. Y.	13½
Dudley, Albany, N. Y.	13
Allegheny, Allegheny, Pa.	13
Rutherford, New York.	13
Ann Arbor University, Ann Arbor, Mich.	12½
Vassar College, Poughkeepsie, N. Y.	12⅓
Morrison, Glasgow, Mo.	12¼
Lick (2), Mt. Hamilton, Cal.	12
Draper, Dobbs Ferry, N. Y.	12
White, Brooklyn, N. Y.	12
Cincinnati, Mt. Lookout, Ohio.	11¼
Middletown, Middletown, Conn.	11

Largest refracting telescope in the world...Lick (California), 36 inches
Largest reflecting telescope in the world......Lord Rosse's, 72 inches
Lord Rosse's telescope is in Ireland.

ADDENDUM

Since chapter on comets was written, a new comet has been discovered (November 16) by Prof. Lewis Swift.

www.ingramcontent.com/pod-product-compliance
Lightning Source LLC
Chambersburg PA
CBHW032147010726
47493CB00008BA/2616